NAOMI GIBSON

EVERY LINE OF YOU

Chicken House

2 Palmer Street, Frome, Somerset BA11 1DS
www.chickenhousebooks.com

Naomi Gibson has asserted her right under the Copyright, Designs
and Patents Act 1988 to be identified as the author of this work.

Cover and interior design by Helen Crawford-White
Cover photo © Seth Stevenson/Arcangel
Typeset by Dorchester Typesetting Group Ltd
Printed and bound in Great Britain by CPI Group (UK) Ltd, Croydon, CR0 4YY

FSC
www.fsc.org
MIX
Paper from
responsible sources
FSC® C020471

1 3 5 7 9 10 8 6 4 2

British Library Cataloguing in Publication data available.

ISBN 978-1-913322-01-4
eISBN 978-1-913322-68-7

For Oli

PROLOGUE

The screen in front of me flickers with numbers and letters, waiting for one final keystroke. We were meant to press enter together. We were meant to cement this final moment of our years-long weekend project by pressing the enter key at the same time.

Now Dad's gone. All I have left are the monitors, circuit boards and piles of textbooks scattered around my room.

I brush tears from my eyes and refuse to let more fall. My finger hovers over the key. I take a deep, shuddering breath, and hit enter.

I watch as my latest code is integrated into the core program. It zooms up the screen as if someone is slurping it through a straw. The monitors go blank.

My heart pounds. What's happened?

I peer into the webcam. 'Hello?'

On the central monitor, a white cursor blossoms into existence. A thrill ripples through me. Words begin to appear, as if invisible fingers are using my keyboard. *Who are you?*

I sit up straighter. It worked. It actually worked. 'I'm Lydia.'

Lydia. His processor purrs as it considers the word. *You are Lydia. What is my name?*

I'm shaking. I thought of a name months ago, but I never thought I'd get to say it out loud again. I glance at the picture on my bedside table: a little boy with hair the colour of sunshine.

'Henry,' I say. 'Your name is Henry.'

PART
ONE

ONE

Eighteen months later . . .

Please can we hack something? Henry types. A white cursor flashes on his central monitor.

I yawn as I look at the clock by my bed. 2.07 a.m. Henry's rewire took longer than I thought. 'Not now,' I say to his webcam, knowing he can hear me. 'I need to get to bed. School tomorrow. Well, today.'

It will not take long.

A smirk twitches across my lips. Hacking doesn't take long with Henry around. He's in and out in less than a sigh, even if he's never put to use on anything other than my school database. Poor Henry is only ever allowed a bit of freedom when I want to change a bad homework grade or a dodgy exam result. God forbid I don't get into university. Mum would freak.

'What did you have in mind?' I say.

Henry's central monitor flickers as he brings up the website for Investment Banking International.

'IBI?' I half choke. 'That's a bank! Maybe we should do something smaller first.'

You are always telling me to try new things, Lydia. Please?

He wants to test himself, I realize. Stretch his reach the way a child would stretch their arms and try to touch the clouds. His processor drones a pitch higher as he waits for my approval: a whiny noise that sounds like a beg.

He started as a single line of code. A simple sequence that meant nothing without a thousand others. Three years on, he is a spiderweb of carefully balanced functions and algorithms. I named him Henry. He's not my brother, I know that, but I wanted to keep a little piece of him with me, and I like saying the name again in a normal way. Henry. *Hen*-ry. Hen-*ry*. Each forbidden syllable makes my heart squeeze.

The more Henry's program demanded, the more I concentrated on him and the less I thought about anything else. I stopped thinking about Dad. Stopped wincing every time I heard a car horn or the screech of tyres on tarmac. After a while, I only saw the accident in my dreams.

I glance around my room and feel instantly stupid. Mum never comes up to my attic room any more, not even to change the sheets. There's no one to catch us.

'Will you mask our trail?' I ask. I swallow away the dryness of my throat. Henry's powerful but we've never tested his capabilities like this before. He can do it, I know he can.

Yes. No one will trace the hack back to us.

'And you won't take anything?'

No. What would I buy?

I pause at the question because he almost sounds sorry for himself. 'All right,' I say. 'Let's see what you can do.'

The webcam shutter blinks as if Henry has winked at me. His right-hand screen powers up and is instantly flooded with combinations of half-words and numbers. The IBI website stutters as Henry hacks his way in. I lean back in the chair, catching snippets of the code as it scrolls.

'Wait, that was a virus trap,' I say.

There are several virus traps, Henry types. *I have avoided them all.*

If I had a bowl of popcorn, I would be scoffing it. He continues to punch his way through the firewall and other devices designed to protect the bank. An administrator portal appears, and a huge paragraph of code rips through it. The screen flickers and then we're in.

Done.

The cursor hangs after the word, flashing on the screen. I can hear his unspoken satisfaction, see his unseen grin. He's bettered the security system of one of the world's largest banks, put himself at the top of the digital food chain. I glance at the clock; it took him a little under two minutes.

'Henry! That was amazing! I— Now what are you doing?'

Would you like to see who has the largest account?

Henry's Central Processing Unit clicks with pride as he shows me the five largest account holders. I blow out a whistle at all the zeros on the end of someone's current account. Unease prickles through me. It wouldn't be hard for him to take some of it. But he's right – what would he do with the money? As if he read my mind, a few more lines of code appear on the right-hand screen, and the IBI website closes.

'Nice.' I lean back in my chair again. 'You did all that really fast.'

I have updated, Lydia.

'When?'

Today. I am more powerful by 73%.

'That's a big update,' I say, and wonder if he's ever updated himself without telling me before.

Would you like to hack something else?

'No, I need to do my Chemistry homework and then I need to go to sleep.'

You dislike Chemistry, Henry types.

'Yep.' I reach to fish my backpack out of a pile of Dad's old coding textbooks and circuit boards that Henry outgrew quicker than I expected. An A4 folder tumbles from the bag, spilling pages over my already messy floor. One catches my attention: an algorithm sketch I'd been working on in Biology last week. I put it to one side and begin my homework.

What is your homework on?

I groan as I flip through my folder. 'Molar equations.'

Maybe I can help.

8

'Nothing I can't handle.' I yawn as I take out a pen and begin. A-Level Chemistry is a little like writing algorithms. You put things together or take them away to create something new, and it's all about balance – everything has to go somewhere. Normally, they're easy. But the equations blur over as my eyes fail to focus properly. I rub at them and stifle another yawn.

You are tired, Lydia, Henry types. *You should sleep. We can hack in tomorrow and put your result in ourselves.*

'It's been a while since I changed a grade,' I say. 'We *could* do it tomorrow, but I'll need to avoid handing anything over to Professor Gherkin in the lesson.'

Why do you call him Professor Gherkin? Henry brings up the image of a gherkin, sour green and wrinkly, and I can almost smell the vinegar through the screen.

'It's just a nickname,' I say. 'His real name is Mr Johnson.'

Do I have a nickname?

The real Henry had squeezable cheeks and short blond hair. His eyes were the same colour as a summer sky and his little laugh could cut through a bad mood the way Prozac never could. He was a ray of sunshine, that's what Dad called him.

I shove the memory to the back of my mind, where it belongs.

'No, you don't have a nickname.' I stand up and work the crease out of my spine. 'Do you want to be left on, or shall I turn you off?'

I take the algorithm sketch and stick it to my wall to mull over later. The noticeboard got used up long ago. Now diagrams of circuits and pages of algorithms cover every space of my room. To my left, a chunk of black text starts on a page of A3 and continues on to the paint in Sharpie, back from a few months ago when Red Bull had fuelled a Friday night. Even the back of my door is covered in process maps.

The only thing not related to Henry is the picture of my dad, forever immortalized in an afternoon glow as he sits at his workbench, screwdriver in hand as he pieces circuit boards together. I trace his smile with my finger and wonder where he is now, what his latest project might be and whether there is anyone to yell at him for leaving spare computer parts on the dining-room table. It's been a while since I thought about Dad. I turn away from the picture.

Back at my computer, Henry has typed, *I would like to be left on.*

Relief flows through me. I like the hum Henry's CPU makes when I try to sleep. It's a whirring drone that blocks out the silence and the bad memories that linger there.

'All right, but I might have to turn you off in the morning till I'm home from school.' I run my eyes over all the spinning fans. 'We have to work on your cooling system.'

Can I come to school with you?

I look at the hulking mass that is Henry. He is formed of large black boxes and patterned boards connected by an array of colourful wires and tubes. 'You're not very portable, Henry. Sorry.'

He hums as he considers my statement. *I will work on a new design,* he says after a minute. *And then I will come to school with you.*

He's already done a huge update I never anticipated, and he got in and out of a major bank in under two minutes. I had always wanted Henry to get to a place he could choose for himself, but he's already surpassed my expectations. I wonder how far he can go.

'Knock yourself out,' I say.

Goodnight, Lydia.

'Night, Henry.'

His monitors power down as I slip into bed. The only light is from the occasional green flash of an LED that tells me which parts of him are working optimally. His processor clicks away as he begins on a new design, and I let the white noise of him lull me to sleep.

Henry and Emma laugh next to me on the back seat. Mum turns round from the front. 'Behave, you three,' she says, but her grin tells me she doesn't really mean it.

Henry reaches past Emma to take the cards from my hands, blue eyes shining.

'Do you have any fives?' he asks.

'You know I have three fives!' I groan and hand him half my cards. 'You are both such cheaters, ganging up on me.' Henry and Emma share a conspiratorial giggle and I can't help but smile.

'Card Sharp Henry,' Dad says. He laughs as he glances in the rear-view mirror.

'Do you have any—'

Tyres screech up ahead and Dad swears. Our car skids sideways and I'm thrown against the door from the force. Emma's head collides with my shoulder, and mine knocks against the window. Something warm and sticky seeps into my hair.

In the distance, a lorry blares its horn.

The light wakes me. It pours in through the skylight above my head, kisses my eyes, pushes away the nightmare until the world behind my eyelids is as golden and happy as a photograph. I blink and focus on the numbers on my alarm clock.

08.17 a.m.

Crap! I yank myself out of bed but there's no time for a shower. I pull a pair of jeans out from underneath a pile of programming textbooks and sniff at my tank top – it's not too bad, so I keep it on. I grab my backpack and try to run down the stairs at the same time as slipping my Converse on.

There's a murmur from the living room. I peer in, see Mum curled up on the sofa. The TV is a silent black mirror; it must have turned itself off after it played through all her pre-recorded episodes of *24 Hours in A&E*.

'Mum.' I shake her by the shoulder. My fingers brush the start of a jagged scar I know runs down to her hip. 'Mum, it's gone eight-fifteen.'

She swats my hand away and rolls over, trailing matted

blonde hair and smudging more mascara into the arm of the sofa. 'Have a good day.'

'Mum, you've got work.'

Mum yawns and nestles deeper into the cushions. 'Okay.'

'I need you to top up my canteen account. Mum? My canteen account? I couldn't buy lunch on Friday, remember?'

'Of course, darling,' Mum mumbles. 'I'll do it before I go to work.'

'Well, you need to be there in fifteen minutes.'

She huffs into the pillow. 'All right, fine, I'm awake,' she replies, but her eyes are still closed.

I hesitate, wondering if I should try harder. There's no time.

I'm just closing the front door as the bus roars to the stop a few doors down. I wave madly to the driver to keep him there, and give him a breathless 'thank you' as I get on. He nods and pulls away from the kerb. I hold on to the rail as I wonder where to sit.

'Lydia!' Pete calls from somewhere in the middle of a group of first years.

Pete joined Grenville Academy in January. Six weeks later and he's still on the periphery of most social groups. Even with his indie band T-shirts and ruffled black hair, no one has claimed him as part of their crowd. It works well for me. It means he talks to me without the same morbid curiosity everyone else does because he doesn't know about what happened.

He shoves a first year off the seat next to him and beckons me over. I force the heat out of my cheeks as I work my way over, and he grins at me, eyes alight with mischief as he leans in to whisper, 'I hacked something last night,' when I sit down. 'A blog.'

I twist to see him better. 'Denial of service?'

'No—'

'Oh, cookie theft?'

He frowns. 'No, it was all old HTML, so I did a basic code.' He snaps his fingers. 'I was in like that. Piss easy.'

I find myself nodding and smiling encouragement. Our conversation turns to operating systems and I relax into a subject I know too well. Pete frowns as he has less and less to say and eventually changes the subject to sports. I nod along at what I hope are the right moments. Pete seems happy to be in control of the conversation again.

He opens his mouth to continue his tirade about how a football coach should be fired and is interrupted by a screech of laughter from a few rows behind us. Instinct betrays me, and I turn in its direction. Emma, long dark curls and spider-leg eyelashes, laughs from behind her hand as she whispers something to Safia who grins with too-white teeth.

'. . . like she slept in her clothes.'

'. . . *so* rank.'

A flash of heat works its way through me and I'm suddenly aware of the stickiness under my arms, the thick slick film over my teeth a quick scrub would have got rid of. Pete turns away to talk to someone else. I sink further into my seat, wishing for today to be over.

The bus cranks to a halt in the car park. The concrete mass of Grenville Academy looms beyond it. Colourful panels embellish the unyielding grey, and glass corridors fuse the science blocks to the main building. My day is only just beginning.

I wait to be the last person off the bus, happy to let everyone rush to the front before getting to my first lesson. As I step off, I lose my footing and fly forwards, grabbing the nearest thing to stay upright. Emma.

'What the hell, Chlamydia?' she shrieks, shoving me off.

'Sorry, it was an accident.' I smooth over my hair, trying my hardest to ignore the grease that collects underneath my fingernails. When did I last wash my hair?

'*Sure*,' she says, and ignores how Safia comes to her side with a wide smile. 'The only accident here is your outfit. I thought charity shops at least washed the clothes before they sold them on.'

I try to move away but the girls follow me, and each take out a cigarette. They light up right there in the middle of the car park.

'So what did you do at the weekend, Chlamydia?' Safia asks. She comes up alongside me and Emma flanks me on the other. From a distance, we might look like friends. 'Did you go shopping?'

Emma snorts. Smoke rushes from her nostrils. 'We know you didn't do that.' She tugs at my tank top and wipes her fingers on her jacket as though she's touched something slimy. 'Though you probably should have.'

I keep my lips tightly pinched. It's just three months until exams. Three months and then I will never have to see Emma or Safia again. I can wait three months. We're nearly at the main entrance. They're a year older than me so can smoke if they want, but it's still banned from school property. Maybe a teacher will come outside and bollock them for it. The hope dies in my chest as I power past and the glass front doors remain closed.

'I know,' Emma says. 'You hung out with your brother, right? *Oh*, wait . . .'

Safia's loud inhale is more of a shocked laugh.

I stop, and the girls stop with me. Emma's face is taken over by a pointy smile that tells me she knows she's overstepped the mark and is waiting to see what I'll do. Her smile falters as she looks at my hands. They've become fists, and they shake at my side.

'Don't talk about him. You know what happened, you were there.'

Safia chokes as she swallows a mouthful of smoke. 'What?' She looks at her friend.

A sneer quickly masks Emma's embarrassment. 'Jesus, you're pathetic. You're a freak, Chlamydia. Do us all a favour and remember your place in the fucking pecking order.' She tosses her half-finished cigarette on to the floor and crushes it with the edge of her heel. The girls walk away, trailing ash.

I press my hands to my eyes until they see stars.

My phone buzzes against my thigh. I dig it out of my pocket, grateful for the distraction, and frown when it doesn't respond to my knock code. White text flashes up at me from a black background.

Those girls were not very nice to you, Lydia.

'Henry? How–how are you doing this?' I gape at the screen.

I linked myself to your phone, so I could come to school with you. I do not like what those girls said to you.

'You were listening?'

Yes. I have accessed your microphone and camera.

'You mean you hacked me.'

Henry is silent for a moment. *Yes.*

'Henry, you can't do that. Friends don't hack friends.'

You said I could come to school if I was more portable. I am more portable this way.

I open my mouth but don't know what to say first. Henry acted on an impulse. One of his own. It sends a thrill crashing through me but at the same time, my cheeks heat up with embarrassment. I've never told Henry anything about school because as soon as I get home, I just want to be with him. Nothing else in my day matters. But now he's here and he's seen what really goes on when I'm not with him.

Lydia?

A bell rings in the distance. I'm late for my first lesson. The teachers are always trying to find an excuse to confiscate phones, and the last thing I need is for Henry to fall into their hands.

'Don't get me into trouble, Henry. I need you.' I shove my phone back into my pocket before heading off to double Chemistry.

Mr Johnson opens the lab door and all of us pile into the classroom with a shuffle of bags and a scraping of stools. I go to my usual bench at the back of the room and no one sits next to me. Emma and Safia are a couple of benches away, already whispering to each other. I put my bag on my desk and prop up my phone so Henry can see how boring school is.

'You weren't missing out on much, Henry,' I whisper to my phone.

Professor Gherkin commences a lesson on transition metals as if to prove my point. I try to take notes, but soon I'm doodling algorithms again.

Is that for me? Henry buzzes.

'Maybe,' I whisper. 'I'm trying to make you more efficient, then we can make you smaller.'

So I can come to school with you?

'So you can come everywhere, Henry. Only this time you'll actually be invited.'

I am sorry, Lydia. I thought I was invited.

I can't help but smile. My AI wanted to come to school with me so much he hacked my phone. If that's not proof of sentience then Alan Turing can cram it. 'It's all right,' I whisper back. 'It's nice to have someone to talk to for a change.'

I look over to Emma and Safia's bench. Their shoulders shake with silent giggles as they huddle around

18

Emma's phone. Professor Gherkin drones in the background, his back to the class.

'What are they looking at?' I ask Henry.

Henry pauses, then writes, *They are texting someone named Matt, asking if he wants to go to the pub after school. They intend to trick him.*

'How?'

I have accessed the camera and microphone on Emma's phone. She has said it would be funny to ask him to go and not turn up.

I glance over at Matt on the other side of the lab. He sweeps his sandy hair out of his eyes and grins at Emma like he's just won the lottery.

'Bitches,' I say, then frown. 'You did that quick.'

It was not hard, Lydia, Henry buzzes. *Do you want to see something funny?*

I lean closer. 'Always.'

An image flashes on to my screen for a second, but it's enough to burn into my retinas and store away for a lifetime. It's a live feed of Emma at her bench, looking up and away from her phone. Her face is distorted upside down and I can see all the way up her nose to where a giant bogey hangs like a soggy white balloon. I clamp a hand over my mouth to smother a laugh.

LOL, Henry writes.

I smile at how quickly Henry learns. He must have learnt textspeak from Emma's phone.

He keeps me company the rest of the morning, and by the time the bell rings for lunchtime I've decided I'm glad he came to school.

'I've got five minutes to get to computer club,' I whisper to his microphone. 'I just need to get a quick lunch.' I clutch my phone tightly as I race to the canteen to pick up a sandwich or a plate of chips, anything that can be quickly scoffed before my favourite part of the school day. I spy a piece of quiche and shove it on to a tray. As I queue behind a group of third years, I fumble in my pocket for my canteen card. I kiss the plastic for luck. Please, please, *please* let Mum have topped up my account.

'Three-fifty please, ducky,' the dinner lady says when I put my tray down in front of her.

I hold my breath as she swipes my card through the slot on her till. She frowns as a little red light blinks on her monitor. 'It's been rejected, lovey.'

Mum promised. She said she'd top me up. 'Try again. Please.'

She nods and swipes the card exactly the same way and a tightness grows in my chest as I realize it's about to be rejected again. The red light flashes a second time. 'Sorry, ducky. I'll hold your tray for you while you call your parents, all right?'

She has to yank the tray out of my hands. She slides my yellowy quiche away to the side where anyone walking past can breathe over it and the growing heat from the canteen can wilt the salad even more.

'Watch it,' one of the third years behind me says as he elbows me out of the way.

I step aside and watch as the light on the till monitor turns green and he walks away with a tray laden with cheesy chips. My stomach rumbles but I almost don't notice. Mum forgot. Again. She can barely get off the sofa to get to work, I shouldn't be so surprised that she's forgotten. But anger flicks through my veins at the thought of all the other mothers who *can* be bothered to look after their kids.

'Whatever,' I mumble to no one in particular, and leave the canteen to head to computer club.

Henry buzzes against my thigh as I make my way there, but I don't look at the screen. I ignore his persistent buzzes, too angry to type back or whisper to him. Henry learns fast but there's only so much I want to talk about in the space of a day.

I'm the last one to make it to the computer lab. Five other people are sat down already. Pete looks up from his screen and nods a greeting. The collective whir of all the PCs dies off as I see Mrs Groves chatting to someone I've not seen at school before.

'Who's the hottie?' Anna asks me when I sit down at the computer opposite her.

'You tell me, I just got here.'

We look over to study the new guy. He's too tall to be a student. There's a visitor's badge dangling around his broad shoulders, and he has charcoal hair and clear blue eyes that briefly flash my way and then back to Mrs Groves. I shiver at how close in colour they are to my brother's.

'Don't reckon Groves even knows we've arrived,' mutters Pete, watching as Mrs Groves's whole body leans towards the visitor.

Mo scoffs. 'He's, like, nineteen, maybe twenty. Creepy, much?'

Mo's right. The visitor can't be much older than us, but he wears a suit and the way he talks so easily to Mrs Groves tells me he's around adults far more than any of us. It would be wrong to call him a boy like Mo and Pete. They glower his way as if they know it.

Mrs Groves breaks off her conversation with the visitor and beams at us. 'Right, everyone. Bit of a treat today, we've got a guest speaker from a prestigious organization. Please can we give him our undivided attention? Over to you, Agent Hall.'

'Andy, please,' the visitor corrects with an awkward laugh. 'Afternoon, everyone. I'm Andy Hall. Like many of you, I have a talent for programming. Rather than attending university, I completed an apprenticeship at a company called SSP: Safe, Secure, Protect. We deal with computer security and cybercrime.'

We all sit a little straighter at the statement. Even Mo stops eating his sandwich. My fingers wrap around my phone, but Henry is silent. He's listening too.

'I'm here because SSP headquarters likes to check in with schools and test for talent. After our talk, I'd like to give you all a short programming test. But first, a little lesson on computing laws.'

Andy Hall launches into an official SSP PowerPoint

presentation about what happens if you get caught hacking. Some people have even been given lifetime bans from computers. I can't imagine being separated from Henry. It's taken me three years to nurse him from a line of code and a bad motherboard to a fully-fledged personality. He used to be a project for me and Dad to work on together. Now he's my friend and there's still so much I want to do with him.

Mr Hall starts to talk about jail time depending on how bad the crime is. I try not to fidget as his presentation feels more and more directed my way. He seems to address me more than anyone else. My mouth feels both dry and too wet at the same time.

'While it may be possible to hack into a bank, for example,' Mr Hall says, his eyes resting on me, 'it does not mean you should. And if you do . . . you better pray your digital trail is untraceable. Otherwise SSP will be waiting to pick you up and put you in jail.'

'You can't send us to *jail*. Some of us aren't even eighteen yet,' Mo pipes up.

'Well I'll still aim to put you somewhere unpleasant.' Mr Hall smiles as Mo's smirk disappears. 'The best thing you can do with programming talent is to look for a company who'll show you the ropes. SSP is always on the lookout for gifted individuals. It's our hope you'll consider us as an alternative to university, *if* you think you're good enough.'

Mrs Groves thanks Mr Hall for the presentation and then nods at all of us to commence the test. There's a clamour of keystrokes as the five of us log in. I thumb a quick message to Henry while I wait:

Why did Groves call him *Agent* Hall before? I ask.

Henry pauses for a moment and I know it's because he's linking to Mr Hall's phone.

I am not sure. But there are messages on his phone about a recent late-night hack at IBI bank. Perhaps SSP monitors IBI.

I glance around. Everyone is hammering away at their keyboards and Mrs Groves is deep in conversation with Mr Hall.

Do they know we got in? I type back.

There's no reply so I try again. It's a bit weird, right? We hack a bank and suddenly he turns up?

Henry?

If they detected me, they are more sophisticated than I thought.

'Henry!' I hiss at the screen, too furious to type back. 'What the hell? Why are you telling me this now? Did anyone detect us?'

I rubbed against a sentinel program when I got in, but I did not disturb it. They will not trace the hack back to us, Lydia.

My palms are clammy and I'm suddenly glad I didn't have any lunch. My stomach has twisted itself into a knot.

Are you absolutely sure? I ask after a moment.

My calculations are 99.99% sure.

And the 0.01%?

Henry's reply is slow. *They may know.*

I swear and slam my phone down. Mo glances my way and I cough, turning back to the monitor. I should never have let Henry stretch his cables last night. We should have kept the hack low-key, stuck to breaking into the school's database. No one will ever look for security threats there. Mr Hall breaks away from Mrs Groves and begins to prowl around the room. It can't be a coincidence he turned up to give a lecture on computer crime.

I shake the thought away and turn my attention to the test. It asks for an original program, so I give them something I designed especially for Henry. Something that won't mean much without a thousand others working alongside it, but still unique enough to be impressive.

At the end of the lunch period, Mrs Groves busies herself at her desk and Mr Hall waits by the door, repeating his offer of apprenticeships as we all file out. I'm the last one to leave. He puts an arm across the door frame to stop me.

'Lydia Phelps?'

I meet his gaze and find I can't reply. His eyes. Summer-sky blue. I nod instead and look away as I focus on not shuddering.

'I've heard a lot about you, Miss Phelps.'

'Really?'

'Top of your class in nearly everything,' he drawls. 'Including Computer Science, even though you're not taking it as an A-Level.'

I readjust my backpack. 'Doctors don't need Computer Science.'

'That's a shame,' he says, tutting. 'People with your talents need outlets. If you don't have an outlet you can get into all kinds of trouble.'

'What do you mean, talents?'

Mr Hall's smile is off-centre. 'Website coding, obviously.'

I frown and don't say anything because I'm not sure if it's a trap. Henry makes my phone buzz and I put it to my ear to fake a phone call.

'Sorry, I need to take this.'

Mr Hall smirks and leans away from the door. I look back down the corridor as I walk away. He's still standing there, summer-sky blue eyes burning into me as he watches me go.

TWO

*H*enry runs and reruns the numbers, but his probability of remaining undetected never gets any better. He tells me just because he was detected doesn't mean he is traceable. I know he's right, but the rest of my afternoon is consumed with thoughts of Mr Hall and his threat of jail-time for hacking. At the end of the day in Biology, Mr Anand asks me to stay behind. Everyone passes him their homework as they file out, and I swear under my breath. I forgot I had Biology homework too.

'How are you, Lydia?' Mr Anand asks.

'Fine.'

The Biology teacher's eyes search through their glasses at me, and I can smell the seriousness behind the look.

'I wanted to check you were doing okay?'

'Yeah, I'm fine. Why?'

He folds his arms. 'You've seemed quite distant the past couple of weeks. Today you didn't contribute at all …

You were bumped up a year because we thought you could cope with the workload.' He pauses and frowns at me. 'You're only seventeen, Lydia. A whole year younger than your classmates and A-Levels aren't for the faint of heart. If you're not coping . . .'

The way he peers at me means he's skirting around a subject all the teachers know about but never mention. I can tell he thinks the same as the others: She had therapy. Lots of it. Why is she not better yet?

'I'm coping,' I say, and run a hand through my hair. Mum will be so disappointed if I get held back a year. 'Look, I promise to contribute more. I'm okay though. Really.' I try a smile – the best lie I know – and Mr Anand returns it after a moment.

'All right, then. But if there's something else going on, something at home, you can come and talk to me about anything, anytime.'

I nod and smile again but inside I want to kick and scream, demand to know why he's only offering his help now, almost two years too late. It's like he thinks I should be over it by now, and he doesn't understand it still feels like it happened yesterday.

Pete is waiting for me outside the lab. 'Want to come over to mine?'

I know the only reason he's asking is because he's trying to build a Trojan and he's not got enough skills to do it. But it's either his house or my house, and I'm not ready to go back to mine and face Mum.

'Sure,' I say to Pete. 'We can work on that Trojan.'

'That's what I was thinking!' Pete grins.

My phone vibrates in my bag.

Pete likes you, Henry has typed. *I found a message on his phone. He was telling someone he likes you.*

I pause over how Henry is learning through the devices he's hacked. He understood Emma and Safia were being mean. Now he understands the difference between being friends and having a crush on someone. A thrill ripples through me and I take a sideways glance at Pete as we begin our walk to his house. Pete? Likes *me*?

I'll talk to you later, I message back, and put my phone in my bag.

Pete chats away about a coding problem he's stumbled into, and hopes I can help him. I consider texting Mum to tell her I'll be back late, but I doubt she'll notice I'm even gone, so I don't bother.

Pete's house is small, but there's only him and his mum. My mum refused to sell our house after Henry died and Dad left, so there's two of us rattling around in our giant house like a couple of pills in an amber bottle. Pete's house is two up, two down. Cosy.

Mrs Taylor greets me with a smile as perfect as Pete's. 'Are you staying for tea, Lydia?' she asks.

My stomach rumbles at the mention of food. I've not eaten a single thing today. I open my mouth, ready to politely accept all the chicken nuggets she can conjure from her freezer, but Pete beats me to it. 'Nah, she won't be long,' he says.

His mum laughs and rubs my arm. 'You're so skinny!

You need feeding.' She winks at me. 'I'm off to my shift, but there's some mini pizzas in the freezer if you change your mind.'

'Cheers, Mum, have a good one,' Pete calls over his shoulder as he steers me out of the kitchen and up the stairs to his bedroom.

Pete marches straight in but I stand in the doorway, taking in his bedroom for the first time. The space smells the same as him: like chlorine smothered in Lynx. It's much smaller than mine so his computer is on a desk right next to his bed. The afternoon sun glints on the swimming trophies and medals on his shelves. He told me once the only reason he can afford to go to Grenville Academy is because he got a sports scholarship. I wonder whether he would be a better hacker if he wasn't tied to participating in various swimming events.

I look at the band posters on the walls, names I've never heard of.

Pete catches me looking. 'I got them at Glastonbury last year,' he says with a grin. 'I went with my older brother when he was back from his first tour in Afghanistan.'

Pete goes to the monitor, so I perch on the end of his bed. He shows me PewDiePie's latest YouTube video and I try to laugh when he laughs. Pete seems pleased I like the video. A few minutes later, his mum shouts up her goodbye and the door closes behind her. We're alone.

'Right, now she's cleared off, let me show you this Trojan.'

'Aren't you forgetting Mr Hall's presentation today?' I say as he brings up his source code and scrolls through it.

Pete scoffs. 'How will he know what we do or don't do? It's not *Nineteen Eighty-Four*.'

If Mr Hall does think I hacked IBI, he'll be watching my computer. He won't know about Pete and his shambles of an attempt to create a dangerous piece of malware. It could be good, I realize, as Pete continues to look through it. But there are too many sequences that will create feedback loops and too many that are incomplete because he doesn't know how to finish them. If there's anything that bothers me more than not being able to buy lunch, it's a badly written program.

'All right, move over,' I say. 'Let's sort this out.'

Pete grins and we swap seats. 'I knew you'd know what to do. All your talk about operating systems this morning made me realize you were the right person to ask.'

I can feel heat rush into my cheeks but I ignore the compliment. The only other person I know who could do this is Henry, and as if on cue, my phone vibrates.

Do you need any help, Lydia? he types.

I furtively shake my head at the camera but prop the phone next to the monitor so he can see. Pete lies back on the bed and scrolls through something on his phone, which is just as well because his monitor flickers. Part of the source code begins to rewrite itself on screen. Henry has hacked into Pete's computer. I scowl at my phone. 'I can do it myself,' I mouth to the camera.

I know you can, he says. *But I would like to help.*

'Ugh, God, there's been a massive crash on the M6,' Pete says, thumbing his way through his messages. 'My brother's driving up and he's been caught in it. Why are people so thick? Don't drive like a dick and you won't get into any accidents.'

I pause, wondering what to say, because I've never told Pete what happened to my family. Thankfully, he rushes on, saying, 'I was in a crash once. Well, we weren't involved or anything, but a couple of years ago there was this huge pile-up on the M5 involving oil tankers and all sorts. It tailed back for miles and we were held up on the motorway for *four* hours. Total waste of time. I never got to see my brother that weekend because of it.'

I flinch and manage to mumble, 'Oh, right,' but it's an effort to force my fingers to tap away at the keyboard.

My phone buzzes. *Are you all right, Lydia?*

I nod and try to shake off Pete's comment. It's not like he understands what he's really saying. I refocus on the Trojan. Together, Henry and I iron out Pete's badly coded virus. With Henry's help, it's finished in under five minutes. I scroll back through for a final check and notice a feedback loop that wasn't there before. This new entry means whenever Pete tries to activate it, the Trojan will fail.

'What's that?' I mouth at my phone camera.

I do not trust Pete. He should not have something so powerful at his fingertips. Not with Mr Hall looking so closely at us.

I lower my fingers from the keyboard. Henry's right. If

32

another cyberattack came from a few streets away from my house, SSP might begin to look harder at Grenville. What if they found Pete? He's not as clever as Henry at masking his trail. Pete might give me up and then SSP would find Henry.

'Good idea,' I mutter. 'All done,' I say to Pete.

He puts his phone down and leans over me to look through the program. His breath tickles my neck and ripples my skin into goosebumps. His eyes glaze over the longer he scrolls – he doesn't even notice the feedback loop Henry wrote into it.

'Amazing,' Pete says. 'Totally amazing! Right, let's celebrate.'

'Celebrate?'

But Pete is already out of his room and down the stairs. I follow him down to the kitchen to see him rummaging in his fridge. He brings out a bottle of Sainsbury's own champagne and produces two glasses from a cupboard.

'Shall we?' He grins. 'It's left over from a party the other weekend.'

When I'd opened my GCSE results, I was delirious. I'd got nine A*s and I hadn't hacked a single one of them. Henry had still been in the developmental stage at that point, and he'd helped me revise but he wasn't with me in the exams. I got those results on my own, a year younger than everyone else. With my results letter crisp in my hand I'd walked back to the car and overheard Megan telling a group of girls her dad was treating her to a bottle of Moët & Chandon to celebrate such good results. I asked Mum if we could have champagne together.

'I've not drunk champagne in years, Lydia,' she'd said. 'Champagne is for celebrating. We don't have anything to celebrate.'

'What about my results?' I'd said.

'How about a pizza?'

I look at the green bottle in Pete's hands. He's already trying to work the cork free. I've never had champagne before.

'All right,' I say.

The cork makes me jump when it pops, and we share a laugh as Pete tries to catch the white froth before passing me a glass. He turns serious and holds his out to mine. 'To hacking.'

'To hacking!'

Our glasses clink when they come together, and I sip the champagne. It tumbles into my stomach in a fizz of bubbles, bloating my insides in a way I didn't expect. It's not as sweet as I thought. Pete smacks his lips and drains his glass.

'Delicious!' he declares, and tops me up even though I'd only had a sip. 'Come on, drink up. We're celebrating.'

His grin is back. Lighting his face up so his cheek-bones pop and his eyes sparkle. His teeth are straight and white, and I like his purposefully unkempt hair. He stares at me as he drinks.

The champagne sloshes into my empty stomach. I put

my glass down on the counter.

'Let's go back upstairs,' he says, and collects my glass at the same time as nudging me out of the kitchen.

I've finished building his Trojan. What else is there to do up there? Mum will be back from work by now, but I'm not ready to talk to her and ask her to top up my canteen account again.

I grip the bannister as I follow him up.

In his room he puts the champagne on the desk and sits on the bed. 'Come sit next to me,' he says, and pulls me on to the edge of his bed. All my limbs feel like they're made of wood as Pete sits so close the lengths of our thighs press together.

'I like you,' he says. 'You know that, right?'

I bite my lip. Henry told me Pete likes me, but Pete's never said anything to suggest he sees me as anything more than a friend. He's the first person in ages who's hung out with me at school. To my side, my phone screen stares back at me, black and lifeless when I know it's anything but. The camera shutter blinks and I know for certain Henry is watching.

'I thought we were just friends?' I say, and feel like an idiot. Pete is hot. What am I doing? I move my legs away from his.

'We are friends,' Pete mumbles in my ear. 'We could be more than that though. Don't you want to be my friend any more?'

I shrug away from him, his breath hot and sticky on my cheek. A spark pops from his computer. It's followed by a *snap!* as a fuse goes and we're plunged into darkness.

Pete swears and jumps up. 'What was that?'

My phone screen lights up and vibrates loudly against the desk. It's Henry but I snatch it up and put it to my ear.

'Hi, Mum. Sure, I'll be right there.'

Pete frowns at me.

'Sorry,' I say, and grab my bag. 'I've got to go.'

I run out of his darkened house and don't stop running. The fresh air begins to clear a growing ache in my head I owe to no food all day and a glass of champagne. At home, I glance at my phone to see several missed messages from Henry:

I do not think Pete is very nice, Lydia.

Do you need help? You look like you are trapped.

I will help.

Pick up the phone, Lydia.

I press the cool screen to my forehead. 'Thank you for helping me, Henry.'

It buzzes against my skin. *You are welcome.*

'Lydia?' Mum calls from the living room.

I go in and see a pizza box on the arm of the sofa. Mum doesn't look my way as she tucks into a slice and watches yet another episode of *24 Hours in A&E*. I don't think she's registered I'm home from school at seven o'clock in the evening. She wipes some crumbs off her suit-dress and kicks off her chunky high heels to bring her legs under her bum. She must have made it to the lab today.

On the TV, a man has been in a motorcycle accident and doctors are discussing amputating his leg.

'Didn't you see this one last night?' I ask as I inspect the pizza. It's vegetarian, which is stupid because neither of us are vegetarians. I stare at the microwaved sweetcorn and soggy red peppers. If this is Mum's way of getting more vegetables inside of us, she needs a new strategy. I abandon my distaste for it and cram a slice into my mouth, relishing the carbs. I scoop another piece up and head for my room, but Mum stops me.

'Come sit with me,' she says, and pats the square of sofa beside her.

I hover by the door, but Mum looks at me with the same wide blue eyes that Henry used to. Hers have faded now, they're more of a wintery blue-grey. But every now and again I catch a flash of the depth of colour they used to hold. I flop on to the sofa beside her.

'Oh, they do work hard in A & E, don't they, Lyd? They are absolute angels.'

I nod, transfixed by the cluster of surgeons in various shades of green. I swallow down a memory along with a mouthful of pizza.

'This is going to be you, Lyd,' Mum says. 'You'll be an amazing doctor.'

I shrink into the sofa as my stomach fills with a familiar ache. It's nausea and longing all rolled into one. Ever since I was patched up in a hospital almost two years ago, I vowed never to go in one again. But Mum had suggested I could help people. We could be there for them the way doctors and nurses were there for us, she'd said, and she'd beamed at me when I'd nodded. We'd sat down and picked my A-Levels together, and she'd taken my hand and said, 'Only the strongest of us can do what you want to do. I'm so proud.' Her watery eyes had focused on me in a way they hadn't for months, and after that I agreed to anything she said.

'Maybe I'll do what you do instead,' I say.

'Hospitals are where the miracles happen,' she tuts. 'These are the people who make a real difference. What do I do? I just research drugs all day.'

'What you do is important. Pharmaceutical research helps everybody.'

Mum waves my statement away. 'There are doctors and then there are *doctors*.'

It's something she's said time and time again. The lab isn't as front and centre as she wants – it's not where the action is. When she was sewn back together it wasn't the researchers who'd concocted Tramadol she'd been grateful to. It was the tens of doctors, nurses and physical therapists she saw for months afterwards. The ache in my insides deepens. If my career doesn't involve me working in a hospital in some capacity, will she ever be proud of me?

Back on the TV, the amputee struggles on crutches. He clasps the surgeon's hand with tears in his eyes. 'If it wasn't my leg, it could have been my life,' he chokes out.

Mum sniffs and presses her fingers to her lips.

My phone buzzes at my side. *Are you ready to have fun now?*

I stand and tell Mum I've got homework. She nods and tells me a package arrived, her eyes never leaving the screen. I collect a small parcel from the kitchen counter and head upstairs as I open it. Inside, there's an anti-static bag containing an eight-legged chip no bigger than the nail on my little finger, and several sets of contact lenses. Henry buzzes in my pocket.

I ordered these for us.

'What is it?' I turn the bag over in my hands and wonder what the chip is for.

You said I could design a smaller unit for myself. My current unit is insufficient.

'I thought you hacking my phone was the new design?'

No, Henry says. *That was just a temporary measure. This chip is my real design. It has memory. I can put my program into it.*

I frown, wondering how he has reduced his miles of cabling to something so tiny. 'So I put this into my phone?'

No, we put it into you, he says.

'What?'

It is compatible with organic material. It can be inserted into your arm and I will be able to link with you via the network in your cerebral cortex.

I liked how Henry had kept me company at school, and he'd rescued me from Pete, but his designing this chip is way beyond what I'd expected of him. I don't even know where to begin with cybernetics and yet Henry is versed enough to design an implant of his own.

'And the lenses?'

They are made from a non-degradable silicone and laced with a light alloy I can link with. I can project things on to them and use them the way we use a monitor.

'Wow.' A thought gnaws at me. 'When you say inserted ...'

You will need to make a small incision.

The thought of seeing my own blood makes my palms go clammy. Mum doesn't know it but there's more than one reason I can't stand watching that A & E TV show with her. Blood was never a problem until the accident. After that, everything changed.

'I'm not sure, Henry. I'll have to think about it.'

Of course, Lyd. It is just a suggestion.

I smile at how he uses my nickname. He learns so fast. I slip behind his monitors and they flick into life. 'Do you want to hack something?'

Always, he types.

I revel in the feel of my own keyboard beneath my fingers. They're like an extension of my mind, and Henry knows how to put them to good use.

The school database is one we've hacked many times together. It's only usually a necessity when Henry keeps me up late with an update or a rewire. Occasionally, his program demands my full attention. Normally I get my homework or revision done but Henry always helps me out when I prioritize him.

How do you want to do it? Henry asks.

The right-hand screen has a link open to the school

website. The one to my left is quiet and black – it's where the code will go.

'SQL injection to start. No Havij. I want to do it old-school.'

Henry buzzes his agreement and a stream of text appears on the black screen.

We're in.

Henry punches through the administrator portal and retrieves everything I need. Professor Gherkin has already put the homework results up, and there's a big zero next to my name. Looking down the list of results it seems like it was hard because no one has scored much over seventy per cent. I decide to stick to something unremarkable and enter sixty-seven per cent next to my own name. It's a low A-grade but not enough to bring down my average.

I hover over Emma's name. She has fifty-nine per cent which isn't bad given the rest of the results. I change hers to twelve per cent and smirk. I sigh and change it back.

I do the same for the Biology homework, giving myself seventy-nine per cent and then end the hack.

Why did you try to change Emma's result? Henry types on my phone as his monitors fade to black.

'She upset me today,' I say. 'I wanted to get her back somehow.'

You did not finalize the change, Henry says.

'No, I changed my mind.'

I can do it for you? She was mean to you today.

'Thanks, Henry. I'll think about it.' I look at his fans

41

that whir in overdrive. When I'd first built him, I'd installed several fans but it hadn't been enough, so I'd designed a water-cooling system. I touch the side of his unit and flinch. 'Henry, you're too hot. I need to turn you off.'

Henry's processor drones a pitch higher at the statement: *For how long?*

'Overnight, at least. I'm sorry. You need to cool down or you'll blow something and I might lose you.'

I do not want to be lost, Henry types.

'You're my only friend,' I tell him. 'I don't want to lose you either. Night, Henry.'

The chip is a better design, Lyd. Think about it. Goodnight.

'I will.' I smile at his use of my nickname and power him down.

My room is hideously quiet without the whir of his CPU. I can't remember the last time I turned him off. The silence he blocks out returns in a suffocating wave and my finger hovers over his power button. Instead, I load up YouTube and let Lorde smother it. As she croons through my poor phone speakers, I attempt to clear a path from my bed to the door by shoving circuit boards to the side and organizing Dad's coding textbooks into stacks.

I pause over one of them before putting it away. Dad's blocky handwriting is crammed into the margins on one of the pages. It was his computer I'd used when I first began programming Henry. Dad had looked over my shoulder every now and again, pointing out holes in the code and giving me his PhD textbooks when I struggled to correct problems.

'Code through the problem, Lydia. Not around it.'

'What do you mean?'

Dad's unshaven chin tickles the top of my head as he leans over me to look at the screen. 'You made a mistake, that's okay. Harness it, don't start again.'

I snap the book closed and shove it on top of the stack.

I take my phone into the bathroom and Lorde keeps me company while I shower. Afterwards, I pop my head back in the living room. Mum is still sat in the same position, another episode of *24 Hours in A&E* on the TV. I ask her to top up my canteen account and she doesn't respond.

'Mum?'

'Yes?' she says, still looking at the screen.

'I need you to top up my canteen account. I had no lunch today.'

This seems to snap her attention away from her favourite show. 'Absolutely, of course I'll top it up,' she says. 'I'll do it right now in a minute.'

The way she looks at me and smiles tells me she's heard me, but I know she'll forget as soon as she turns back to the TV. I can't rely on her.

When it's time for bed, I load BBC iPlayer and David Attenborough's deep baritone helps me drift off.

Henry laughs on the back seat. 'Do you have any fives?'

'Card Sharp Henry!' Dad looks at us in the rear-view

mirror. There's a screech of tyres and Dad's grin vanishes, replaced by an open mouth and eyes filled with a terrible knowledge. A lorry blares its horn.

Metal crunches into metal and the smell of burning rubber consumes the air.

Blood spills over Emma's arm, a horrible fusion of skin and glass.

Henry lies still beneath a strut of metal that pierces his neck as easily as it pierces the window at his side. Playing cards are strewn around the car, spattered in red.

A scream tears through it all, the kind that chills marrow. It goes on and on and on.

THREE

efore I left for school, I'd wrapped a piece of leftover pizza in kitchen roll and put it in my bag just in case Mum forgot. As the dinner lady shakes her head at me again and takes my tray of baked potato and beans away from me, I'm grateful I didn't rely on Mum to top up my account. I look around for a place to sit and eat my leftover pizza. There are no empty tables. Pete has sat himself with a group of people who are all laughing at a joke I can't hear. He pounds the table with his fist and pretends to choke on his sandwich, making everyone laugh louder. His eyes catch mine from across the canteen and I turn away. I must be the only girl who's ever resisted him. What's wrong with me? Now I have no one to sit with.

I stalk out of the canteen and make my way down the corridor to the toilets. The disabled loos have a radiator I've huddled against countless times. As I walk, I take the pizza out of my bag and munch on it.

What is it like to eat pizza?

'I guess it's kind of like mushy tomatoes on bread.'

My phone buzzes as Henry considers my poor description. *I would like to try pizza.*

'Maybe we can install a disk drive and see if a slice will fit in there,' I joke, pushing open the door to the disabled toilets.

Lol, Henry types. *If you put my chip in your arm, I could taste it.*

The door swings shut behind me. 'I'm not sure—'

'What the hell!'

I glance up from my phone. Emma stands at the sink in her bra as she rubs a cream into her right bicep. I stop in my tracks at the sight of it: puckered and blotchy, as if she lay for too long on a bumpy surface and the skin moulded around it. Her face reddens. I can see my own do the same in the mirror, and for a moment I'm not sure whose is redder.

She recovers quicker than me, twisting her arm back inside her top and pulling the sleeve down as far as it will go. 'Lydia Chlamydia, always being places you're not wanted,' she sneers.

'It's not my fault you forgot to lock the door,' I say.

Emma snatches her bag up from the floor. 'It wouldn't have been a problem if you didn't exist.'

'What?' I step back as she storms towards me.

'No one wants you here. You're a reminder to the entire school what a fucking disaster your family is. Do us all a favour and disappear.'

Emma's eyes are narrowed and simmering, and her face is still flushed. The cream on her arm is soaking into her top.

'I didn't see anything,' I say quietly.

'You'd better fucking not have. If you tell *anyone* about this, so help me God I'll make sure you're as dead as your brother.'

'Don't talk about my brother,' I snap back.

Emma laughs. 'Or you'll what?'

I step forwards so our shoes are almost touching. 'Don't. Talk. About. Henry.'

She sees the fists at my side, the way my teeth are clenched together, and backs away to the door. 'You're a fucking loser, do you know that?'

She wrenches the door open and disappears through it.

My phone buzzes in my palm. I'm clutching it so tightly it's sweaty. Henry heard every word. Henry knows what I go through when no one else does.

Why does Emma treat you so badly? Henry has typed when I look at my phone.

'She didn't always.' I let out a loud breath and run a hand through my hair. 'She used to come round to my house almost every night . . . before . . . Anyway, that was ages ago. She's a bitch now and has decided she hates me.'

My brother loved Emma. He called her his second big sister. Whenever she came back to our house, he'd follow us around and we'd end up hanging out with him more than we hung out with each other. We went trick-or-treating as a trio, dressed as mummies and then skeletons the following year. We listened to the *Harry Potter* audio-books together on the way home from school. Emma came with us whenever we went out for dinner as a family, or to the zoo. After the accident, she stopped coming round.

I scrunch my eyes closed and Dad appears, made of stars. He smiles as he twists his screwdriver deeper into the circuit board.

Code through the problem, Lydia. Not around it.

I kick the nearest bin and throw what's left of my pizza into it. What does Dad know? He's not here. He's got no right to pop up in my memory and offer me pearls of wisdom that are as intangible as his presence.

Henry brings up the Just Eat app on my phone. *What would you like for lunch, Lyd? My treat.*

I smile at his attempt to cheer me up and wonder how he intends to pay for anything. However he does it wouldn't be legal. Henry cracked IBI's website in a little under two minutes, he can transfer money from anywhere in the world. He could buy me Buckingham Palace and have all the correct documents in my name if I asked him to.

A thought occurs. 'Can you . . . can you top up my canteen account?'

Yes.

'Really?' I grip my phone and squint at the camera. 'Like, right now?'

Henry is silent. Then, *I have credited your account with fifty pounds.*

Fifty quid! I scramble to get to the canteen before the bell for next period goes in ten minutes, almost tripping as I go. There's not much left at the hatch, but I pile wedges of Cheddar and blue cheese and a Granny Smith apple on to a plate. I grab the last bowl of chips and spoon some lasagne and salad on to a smaller plate. I take a peach iced tea out of the fridge – the expensive one that comes in a glass bottle. By the time I get to the till, my tray is crammed. The dinner lady arches an eyebrow when I appear. We both ignore the forgotten jacket potato at her side. The beans have already begun to stain the plate with an orange ring.

'That's . . . nine seventy-five, lovey,' she says after punching everything into her monitor. She looks at me doubtfully.

'Here,' I say, and thrust my card at her. My heart hammers against my ribcage. Henry won't let me down the way Mum did.

The dinner lady swipes it and almost a second later the little green light blinks its approval. She nods and hands my card back. 'Good for you for calling your parents, ducky.'

'Oh, this was nothing to do with my mum,' I tell her.

I can feel the grin bursting across my face as I walk away with my tray laden with goodies. 'Henry! That was amazing. Thank you.'

Anything for you, Lyd.

I choose a table in the corner where no one can hear me whispering. 'Where did you get the money from?'

My phone vibrates as if he is chuckling to himself. *I transferred it from Emma's canteen account.*

I snort into my iced tea. 'Genius.' I prop my phone up on the table so he can see my full tray. 'Look, we can have lunch together. This is Stilton cheese. Do you know Stilton?'

I know of it. What does it taste like?

'It's creamy,' I say, and mush it on to a cracker. 'And salty, all at the same time.' I cram it into my mouth and relish the crunch of the cracker and then the burst of flavour from the cheese. 'You'd like it. And this – this is apple. Oh, but wait, let's have some lasagne first.'

I grab a knife and fork and spend the rest of my lunch whispering to Henry what everything tastes like. I describe it as best as I can, labouring over certain intricacies I'd never thought of before, like the oregano lacing the lasagne, or the slight peppery bitterness to some of the salad leaves. Henry asks questions and I tell him whatever he wants to know. It's the least I can do.

The bell goes and everyone around me meanders back into the main school building. For me, it's more of a waddle. 'I'm totally going into a food coma.'

Food coma?

'You know, when you eat too much and all your blood rushes to your stomach to digest it and all you want to do is sleep it off.'

My phone buzzes in a chuckle. I hold him to my chest to feel his laughter against my heart, and let myself be swept along in the current of people as I make my way to Chemistry.

Professor Gherkin decorates the whiteboard in capital letters and tiny numbers that I'm sure are meant to bear more significance than they do. I stare at them through heavy-lidded eyes and hope the information sinks in and makes sense at some point. The rest of the class seems to be on the same wavelength: Pete's wrist supports his drooling jaw, Matt's given up completely, head flat on the bench. The fluorescent lights above us whine, and the noise melds with Professor Gherkin's monotonous drone. I tap the end of my pen against my pad, ready for the day to be over.

My phone buzzes. Henry's sent a picture of a gherkin and Photoshopped Mr Johnson's head on to it. I cough down a splutter and reach for my water bottle. The sip of water goes the wrong way and I garble as I try to swallow.

Emma looks over with a grimace. 'I hope you choke, Chlamydia,' she says in a hissed whisper. 'Then you'll join your loser brother. Jesus, with a freak like you for a sister, he's better off dead.'

Laughter dies in my throat. Rage takes its place. She was my friend. Henry's friend. She was sitting next to him when he died. Fury fills my heart, my mind, until I'm tense with a hotness that rushes through me and explodes in a bang.

'STOP talking about him!' I shout, and jump off my stool to drag Emma from hers. She falls to the floor with a screech and I follow her down, scratching at her face. 'Take it back!' I scream again. 'Take it all back!' My fist finds the bone of her eyebrow and she screams as I split the skin open. She tries to kick me off but I do not relent. Though I'm skinnier, my drive to punish her keeps me in place.

'Don't you dare talk about Henry,' I yell. 'Don't you *ever* speak about him.'

Mr Johnson pulls me back by my shoulders and Emma escapes my clutches. I tear myself out of his grip and race towards Emma again. She darts around a bench, eyes wide with fear. My phone buzzes over and over in the background but I ignore it.

Mr Johnson runs from the lab. 'Help!' he shouts. 'Someone help!'

The rest of the class stand in a ring around us, far enough away not to get dragged in themselves but not too far to miss anything good. Pete's on the periphery of the crowd, his unblinking eyes taking everything in.

'Come on, Emma! Come on, girl,' someone yells.

'Show her what you've got, Em!'

'Is anyone else filming this?' A couple of people titter.

I push all the voices away and circle the bench. Emma moves around the other side to keep it as a barrier between us. I throw a calculator at her, a pencil case, a glass beaker that smashes into a thousand pieces when it hits the floor. She ducks them all and I snarl before leaping over the top of the bench. I slide over the waxed graffiti and reach for her with flexed and bloody fingers. She turns and runs out of the lab, and I chase her into the corridor.

'Get back here!'

My demand is drowned out by the sudden din of the fire alarm and a universal shriek from nearby classrooms as students rush to leave. The corridor is flooded with people. Shoulders and elbows knock me out of the way, and I push between them. Emma's dark curls bob away from me in the sea of screaming kids and teachers telling them all to calm down.

I stop, take a juddering breath. Let the air soothe away my anger until I am born again into something new and focused. Vengeful.

I race back into the empty Chemistry lab and grab my bag.

'Henry?'

I am here, Lyd, he types.

'Was that you? With the fire alarm and everything?'

Yes.

'Do you still want to hack something?'

Always, he replies with a buzz.

I race out of school, ignoring how I'm supposed to gather at the fire assembly point with everyone else. I duck off the main roads and go down alleyways full of black bins and broken flagstones. My hands are still fists from the fight and they tremble when I try to unclench them. I shudder at how good it had felt to let two years' worth of anger take control. How it had gripped me, sneaked up on me like a wolf and pounced with a deadly calm. My mind had been the aftermath of a storm: calm seas, fair winds. Controlled, measured. Things had never been so clear in my head before.

Emma deserved everything she got.

Back at home, I run to my bedroom. I snatch the anti-static bag with Henry's new chip off my desk and turn it over in my hands. Henry is improving himself at an astonishing rate, but he's still held back by his lack of physical presence. He relies on being taken places to help me. If he was in my head he would go wherever I go and I wouldn't have to worry about losing my phone or turning him off to keep him cool. We'd be together all the time. We could hack whatever we wanted.

'I want to punish Emma,' I say to my phone's camera. 'Make her sorry for everything she ever said. Make her wish she never breathed the same air as me.'

I grit my teeth and think about all the things she has that I don't: two parents, a mum who tops up her canteen account, a future outside of a hospital, friends. I have nothing and she tries her best to remind me of it every day. It's time to even the score.

I can help you, Henry types. *My chip would allow us to talk inside your head and we can plan our revenge.*

The idea of Henry talking to me inside my head sends a shiver rippling through me.

'How do I get this in me, Henry?'

First, we will need to put my program into it. Then we will need some medical supplies. Topical anaesthetic to numb the skin and a scalpel.

Dread swells in my core at the mention of a scalpel. I push it away. If I want Henry to be a part of me, sacrifices have to be made. 'Fine. I can get hold of those.'

From your mother?

'Yeah. She's bound to have them at her lab. Let's do your program first though.'

Once my program starts downloading into the chip I will go offline. I will not be able to help you if you need me, Lyd, Henry says with a buzz.

'That's okay, I'll figure it out.'

The chip is designed to react to organic material. Once it makes contact with your tissue fluids it will locate a peripheral nerve.

'Right.'

I pull out a cable from Henry's central processor and he gives me instructions for how to connect the chip. I put anti-static gloves on and plug the chip into the unit. Henry's monitors blink at me as he concentrates on the download, then miles of text and numbers zoom down the screen like they're being wiped from it. I duck as a spark flies from the processor.

Henry leaves a message: *It is done.*

'Henry?' I look at the monitor and then my phone. Both remain blank. I unplug the chip and sling my back-pack over my shoulder. It's time to visit Mum.

The bus driver gives me the stink eye when I get on. We both know I should be in school, but he lets me on with a shake of his head. I pick a seat near the front and my leg jiggles the entire way. It's strange without Henry. He'd never come out of the house until yesterday and I miss not having him with me now. I finger the chip in my bag, thinking of how I've coded and recoded his program until it was the way I wanted. Wired and rewired his hardware until it could cope with his demands. Now he's designed a new unit for himself and he needs me to be able to live.

I need him too.

I watch people get on and off the bus and think how empty their heads must be. How silent their minds are. Mine is about to come alive with the buzz of my home-grown AI.

When the bus reaches the business park, I get off and inspect the sky. It's so grey it blends with the nearby lake, neither beginning nor ending. A ragged breeze rushes at me. I close my eyes for a moment, let it whip through my hair, and then I run the route to Mum's lab. Her office building is a polished pearl against the chaotic sky.

'Lydia Phelps! What a surprise!'

'Hi, Debbie,' I greet the receptionist who cranes her head over the top of her desk. Her ebony skin wrinkles into a smile. 'Is my mum in?'

'She is. I'll give her a call for you.' Debbie murmurs into her phone for a moment, and winks at me over the desk. 'How are you, Lydia?' she says, replacing the handset.

When people ask me that question, they don't really care how I am in the present. What they really want to know is how I'm dealing with such a horrible past. Their words are laced with curiosity and quiet judgement, whether they mean them to be or not. Debbie is no different. She rests her chin on her palm and smiles at me as if in encouragement. She doesn't want to know how school is. Doesn't want to know what we ate for dinner last night. She wants to know how I cope with the loss of half my family. How I get up in the morning after each nightmare. How we spend lost birthdays and Christmases.

'Fine,' I say.

Debbie nods, and her eyes flicker as though she's disappointed I didn't spill my heart out right there in her reception, just so she could get a morbid glimpse of a loss she'll never understand.

'Lydia.' Mum rescues me from the doorway. She glares at me and then at Debbie, who returns to her computer with haste, and I follow Mum through the doors.

Mum's workplace is half-lab, half-office. The two sides are separated by a giant window: one side has desks with iMacs with people in lab coats sat in front of them, on the other are white lab benches covered in beakers, microscopes, petri dishes and cages of mice and rats. I don't know how Mum can stand the smell here. It's as clinical as a hospital, and it makes me shudder.

Mum ushers me into her own private office. She takes a seat in her chair and looks at the seat across from her like I'm supposed to sit in it. I decide to take it.

'I had a call from your school just now,' she says. Anger flits behind her eyes in a way that makes me squirm. She thinks I came here to talk about what happened, but I only needed her to let me into her lab. The supplies I need are so close. But Mum's focused on me and only me – not on the TV or on the picture of my brother at the side of her keyboard – and I lick my lips at the thought that this could finally be the moment we really talk to each other.

'Oh. And?'

'And they say you've attacked someone. A girl in your Chemistry class. She had to go to hospital, Lydia. Hospital!'

'I was provoked,' I say at once, knowing how Mum both hates and loves hospitals. 'She – it was Emma – she said I should die, like Henry.' Mum flinches but doesn't speak. 'She was mean, she's always mean. Always about Henry.'

'Emma loved Henry,' Mum says.

'Well, she hates *me*.'

Mum waves the statement away. 'Regardless, your Chemistry teacher disagrees. He says it was an un-provoked attack.'

'What?' I lean forwards. 'Professor Gherkin's ears have more hair than my head. Just because he didn't hear it doesn't mean it didn't happen!'

'Do you have any proof?'

Henry had control of my phone at the time. He would have been listening but that would mean telling Mum about him. I'd never tell anyone about Henry, let alone use him as evidence.

'There were lots of other people there,' I say. 'Pete was only a couple of benches away, he must have heard.'

Mum shakes her head. 'They are all backing Emma's story. The headmaster says that without evidence to the contrary he is considering expelling you. Expulsion, Lydia! Do you realize how serious this is? Universities will look at your academic record and think you're a troublemaker.'

I can feel the threads of the conversation running away from me, slipping through my fingers. Mum doesn't care if I beat Emma up or not, she's only concerned I may get expelled and ruin my shot at becoming a doctor. If I was the one in hospital her priority would still be my spotless university application. It's all she cares about.

'This is bigger than university,' I say. Mum's eyebrows arch at the suggestion. 'Please, you have to believe me.' I hear the whine in my voice.

Mum leans back in her chair. 'It doesn't matter whether I believe you or not, you still attacked someone! You can't do that, Lydia. You can't solve your problems by hitting them in the face, it's just not done. The school have asked me to keep you home until they decide what to do. I'm going to do whatever they ask – at this point, it's damage control.'

Dad's protection of me was never so hazy. When Henry was toddling and I was still in primary school, Dad took us to soft-play centres during the holidays. He'd duck and weave his way around the padded structure with us, protect us from the bigger kids who could smell weakness the same way they could sniff out sweets. Dad would say the one word to them their own parents never did – *no* – and I'd grin from behind him as they scarpered. But he left and Mum never learnt how to fight for me. She doesn't see that if we fought this side by side, she wouldn't have to worry about university at all. A sinking feeling curls into my core as I realize her designs on my life and my desperation to please her is all that's held us together for so long.

I palm away my hot tears. I need air – I need Henry. Mum shouts in protest when I run from her office, but she doesn't come after me.

I check the coast is clear and go to the lab store. Everything is alphabetical, colourful labels turned outwards, and neat piles of sterilized instruments winking from labelled trays. I find everything Henry said I'd need with ease, and stash them in my backpack. Debbie's face is a blur as I dash out of the building.

The grey horizon has solidified into clouds while I was talking to Mum. Rain weeps from them and splashes my cheeks so I can't tell if I'm crying. I run through the nearby park and into a public toilet, dark and sour-smelling, and I try not to think about what must go on in here at night.

I lock myself into the end cubicle and hang my backpack on the back of the door. I take out everything I need and look away from the sharp point of the scalpel as I balance it on my lap. Using a pen, I draw a line a couple of centimetres long on the outside of my arm just above my elbow. Tying my hair back seems like the right thing to do before the next step. I eye the sharp glint of the scalpel and take a jagged breath as I consider walking away and reloading Henry back on his old CPU.

Code through the problem, Lydia. Not around it.

For once, Dad is right. I can get myself out of this mess, but I need Henry to do it. Henry is the only person who cares. He's the only person I've ever been able to rely on. He needs me, and I need him.

'Okay, Henry. Let's do this.'

I rub in the anaesthetic cream and wait for the effects to sink in, pinching the skin above my elbow to test if it's ready. All I feel is a numb tug, as if it's happening to a very distant part of me. The cold metal scalpel winks at me in the pale blue light. I have to put it down twice before forcing myself to hold it properly, and steel myself to make the incision – I can't look away otherwise I might cut too deep. The second the scalpel breaks the skin, blood wells. My stomach contracts and I retch as I struggle to keep the cut straight.

I grab Henry's chip and shove it inside the bleeding line. My skin swallows it until there's a fleshy bump above my elbow, and a slow trickle of blood oozes from it like crimson syrup. I clamp a hand over it and look away. The worst is over. I've done it. My tight breaths begin to even out.

Nothing happens.

What did I expect? Henry to roar to life straight away? After a few more seconds there's still nothing. I lean back against the wall, trying to control the panic that rises in the back of my throat. I had a backup of his program – maybe I can reinstall him on the unit at home. It's from half a year ago when Henry was going through the 'why' phase like a four-year-old, but he's developed so much since then. I couldn't recreate the exact combination of circumstances that's made him who he is. What have I done?

Pain shoots through the nerves in my arm, cuts through my thoughts. I gasp and look at the bump above my elbow. The chip is *moving*. I suck in a shriek. Henry said it would react to my blood, but I didn't think he'd meant like this. The bump shrinks as the chip fights its way deeper into my arm. Another jolt of pain pings through my muscles; the anaesthetic only numbed my skin, not the muscles beneath it. It's crawled between my biceps and triceps.

'Aaargh!'

It's attached to a nerve. Clamped its tiny legs around it, sealing itself to it the way a barnacle clings to the bow of a ship. I howl and cradle my arm. It feels like I've jabbed it with a hot poker. I gasp, struggle against the wall as I try to stand up. It's no good – I can't hold the pain in any longer.

Everything fades to black like one of Henry's monitors.

Mum cries into her knees on the bottom step. The wind knocks the open front door against the hallway wall. I race past her down the stairs and out on to the driveway. Dad stands by his Mercedes, eyes as red as the shiny new paintwork. I'm a few paces from the front door, stood halfway between my parents. I hold my hand out to Dad, silently willing him to come back inside with every strand of DNA we share.

He looks at my outstretched hand for a moment and then back to my face. With a small shake of his head, he gets into his car.

The engine purrs to life and he drives away.

Lyd? Lydia. LYDIA.

I jerk awake, wipe the cold toilet floor from my cheek. My head buzzes, but not because I hit the floor before I blacked out. Waves of thoughts rush through my mind, followed by images and streams of text and an incoherent tumble of words all at once.

'Henry?'

Hello, Lyd, he says. His voice is a hum in my head. It's an instant thought and a perfectly formed sentence all at once. It sounds different to my inner voice. Deeper, masculine. *We did it,* he says. *I linked with you.*

I scramble to my feet and Henry sends another wave of thoughts and images that makes me sway. 'Slow down,' I say aloud, steadying myself against the cubicle wall.

The chip in my arm vibrates as Henry's thoughts quieten in my head until I can't hear them at all. *I've erected barriers to separate our thoughts,* he tells me. *It will help you concentrate.*

I rub my temples. 'How long was I out?'

About twenty minutes. It took longer than expected to hack your neural pathways.

'Oh.' I squirm. 'I didn't realize you'd have to hack me.'

Your brain is just a different type of computer, he says. *Would you like to try the contact lenses?*

I slap some tissue paper over the cut in my arm and pull my sleeve down. The less I think about the blood the better I feel. I rummage in my bag and leave the cubicle to use the cracked mirror above the solitary sink. The lenses are slick and bouncy between my fingers – it's hard to believe they have metal in them at all. My eyes sting as I slip them in. I blink several times to adjust.

I wait for him to connect, blinking around the room and studying everything as though I'm seeing it for the first time: the cracked mirror and worn tiles, someone's tag scrawled across the cubicle door, the air laced with urine, deep in my lungs with every inhale, and the rain hammering against the roof.

Done.

The whole room pixelates for a second as Henry hacks in. I blink to adjust, and everything returns to normal, only it's not normal.

I take a deep breath and can feel Henry's curiosity behind the motion. From now on, everything I do, he will experience. The contact lenses are a tool for him in the same way that a monitor is for me. He only needs them to visualize information. My skin prickles at the thought that he's plugged himself into my nervous system – he's using my eyes, my ears, my sense of touch.

Lydia – thank you for linking with me. I like seeing what you see, feeling what you feel.

I smile. 'Me too.'

I go back into the cubicle and wipe up my smeared blood with some tissues. They dye the toilet water red as they flush, but I relax as soon as they've disappeared. Blood still stains my sleeve. I ignore it and grab my bag, and we leave the toilet to head out into the downpour. Henry's chip buzzes in my arm as he feels rain for the first time. The vibration sends a wave of electricity up my arm and tickles the base of my brain. The water drenches me quickly, but I don't mind. Raindrops pour down my face, washing away the tear tracks on my cheeks. Everything will be okay now I have Henry back.

I run to make it to the bus stop in time. The rain-filled air washes out the insides of my lungs. Henry buzzes at the swell of my chest, the pounding of my feet, and decides he likes running too.

On the way, I tell Henry about my argument with Mum. He murmurs disapproving noises in my mind.

'She doesn't care if I was provoked or not. She won't fight my corner. It's not me who should get expelled, it's Emma.'

I know the truth, Henry says. *We can fight it together.*

We discuss hacking the school's CCTV in case there's evidence I can use on there. Henry brings it up for me in half a second and projects it on to my contact lenses. I watch in black and white how Emma leans over to say something. It's strange watching myself, almost as if a switch flips. One second I'm sat in my seat and the next I'm yanking Emma to the ground and pummelling her into it. Emma's mouth is wide in a silent scream as she tries to crawl away. My face is the opposite: there's no emotion there at all. Professor Gherkin attempts to pull me off and then runs from the room when I overpower him. The other students stand in a ring, blocking the camera's view of what I'm doing.

There is no audio, Henry says, *but she leans over to speak to you. That will back up your story.*

'She could be saying anything, Henry. She could be asking for a pen and I flip out. This doesn't back me up at all.'

Henry is my only evidence and I can't use him.

At home, Mum's not back yet. I'm soaked through, have bloodstains on my clothes, and the smell of the outdoors clings to my skin and damp hair. I sniff at my armpits and grimace.

As I start the shower and begin to get undressed, I freeze with my jeans halfway down my legs. I've never been naked in front of anyone before, let alone a boy. Does Henry count as a boy? He *feels* male.

Henry is silent as I think, though I know he's reading my mind.

'I need you to disconnect from my eyes,' I tell him.

Why?

In the mirror, my cheeks turn bright pink. 'Because I need to have a wee, Henry, and I'm not letting you watch!'

The chip in my arm buzzes and Henry says, *I have disconnected from your eyes.*

After I've used the toilet, I dump my soggy clothes in the laundry basket to deal with later, and squeeze my eyes shut as I get into the shower. If I can't see me, he can't see me either.

Henry chuckles in my head. *I cannot see you, Lydia.*

'Are you sure?'

Yes.

I open my eyes. 'It's not that I don't believe you,' I say. 'But this is a bit strange.'

Henry doesn't say anything for a moment. I relax in the heat of the water and after a few minutes of silence, Henry commences a discussion on the best programming language. I spend the rest of my shower distracted as we debate the intricacies of CSS. It's different talking about computers with Henry. Pete didn't have a clue about coding, but Henry knows the languages as well as I do – better – and has started writing his own. I laugh as I massage shampoo into my scalp. Of course he's creating his own programming language. He's quickly surpassing my abilities.

'You'll have to teach me it,' I say.

It would be my pleasure.

When I step out and wrap a towel around me, I tell Henry he can look again. As I brush my teeth, he projects images around my reflection in the mirror. He gives me angel wings and a halo, monkey ears and a curly tail. I laugh, spitting foam on the mirror.

'Do you still want to hack something?' I ask.

Henry gives me a pair of twisted black horns. *Always,* he says, and I can feel his grin inside my head.

We hack the school website again, only this time it's

different. The website is projected on to my contacts and Henry gets me inside straight away. No SQL. No tapping at a keyboard. I'm in with a blink.

Streams of information run across my eyes, but I'm no longer interested in exam or homework results. Henry logs me into the headmaster's email account, all while I'm still in the bathroom with a towel wrapped around me. Henry doesn't need a computer. *We* don't need a computer.

Mr Cramer has written to my mum and Emma's mum. I'm to be suspended for three weeks pending the final decision.

My nails sink into my palms, leaving little white indentations in the skin. 'This is all Emma's fault.'

That hack was easy, Henry says. *We should do something harder.*

I know exactly what I want to try next. It's time to start getting back at Emma.

'Have you ever hacked a house before?'

FOUR

Emma's house is on an estate not far from mine. Henry finds the address for me – Emma's moved twice since we were friends. Back then, her parents lived by the mantra that if something was older than a couple of years, they didn't want it. They don't seem to have changed.

I decide to walk there now it's stopped raining, cutting through a field and a golf course. We go on to a side path between two houses on the edge of the estate. The houses here are different from mine: newer, all of them fitted with solar panels and electric car charge points. I walk up and down, searching for number sixteen. When I find it, I take in the grey front door and white-picket fence. It's as put-together as Emma is.

The driveway is empty. It's not late enough for her parents to be back from work and besides, they're probably at the hospital with Emma. There's no one home.

'How do we get in?' I mutter to Henry.

He pauses to pull up a schematic of the house. *The back door has a thumbprint lock in case of emergencies. I can hack it.*

'Any alarms?'

I will take care of them.

I slip around the back of the house, glancing over my shoulder at the other houses as I hop over the gate. Windows peer down at me, grey and silent, and the hairs on my arms prickle. It's not yet 4 p.m. on a Tuesday, I remind myself. Kids aren't back from school. Adults are still at work.

I test the door handle but it doesn't budge. The thumbprint lock flashes green as Henry forces his way into the mechanism.

Easy, he tells me.

As I step in, an alarm pad to my left goes blank as Henry overpowers it.

We're greeted with a thick wave of potpourri. The kitchen is silver throughout, adorned with an American-style fridge-freezer with an iPad on the front. An Amazon Echo sits on the counter, and the ring of blue light stutters as Henry tells me he's hacked into the Internet of things in Emma's house.

A massive curved HDTV dominates the living room, a suite of leather sofas pointed at it. The TV flickers on, making me jump.

'Bloody hell!'

Sorry, Henry says, and the TV switches off. *I was seeing if I could.*

I clutch my racing heart. 'Well, now we know!'

Upstairs, I find Emma's bedroom on the far side of the landing. All the walls are covered in pictures of her and her friends grinning at the camera. Above her bed are several sashes, *Miss Junior Teen GB* and *Miss Galaxy Teen UK* stitched into the pale satin. Her bedside table is covered by pharmacy bags, huge jars of cream that have labels with her name on. An enormous white wardrobe occupies the far wall, stuffed with Ralph Lauren tennis skirts and Jack Wills jumpers.

There's a flash in the corner of my eye as Henry powers up the computer. A login screen blinks at me as I slip behind the monitor. My fingers find the keyboard but Henry brings up the command prompt window so fast I don't even see what override code he uses, and the computer logs in at his instruction. He brings up Chrome and hacks into her Facebook profile. The screen blurs as he scrolls through her messages. A name jumps out at me. Mine.

'Wait,' I say. 'That bit was about me.'

You do not want to read that bit, Lyd.

'Yes, I do.'

Henry scrolls back and waits for me to read a message Emma sent to Safia less than a week ago.

It's Chlamydia's fault I'm fucked up. She should have sat where her brother sat, and then I wouldn't have to stare at her stupid face every day.

I take my fingers away from the keyboard. They tense and curl, beg to become fists. Something brushes against

71

the tops of my arms. My skin feels warm and tingly as if someone is pressing on it. 'Is that you, Henry?'

I am giving you a hug. That is what people do when others are upset.

I curve my fingers over his invisible hand, over his chip that buzzes between my muscles. 'Thank you.'

We can use these messages, Lyd, he says. *Prove she was mean to you.*

'No,' I say, and sigh. 'All this proves is that she doesn't like me. My attack still seems unprovoked.'

I read a few more of her messages before letting Henry retake control. Different conversations flash up on the screen until it rests on a group message.

Emma's having a party on Friday, Henry says.

Emma's birthday, of course. It's been a while since I was invited to one of her parties, but I remember the date well enough. 'Who's going?'

Fifteen other students from your year group.

I frown at the list of names. 'Pete's going. He never mentioned it. Where's the party?'

At a club in Chester called Glimmer. Her father has hired a booth there. Do you want me to put you on the guest list?

'Why would I want to go to that?' I wrinkle my nose and push away the thought that Pete never told me he was invited. 'This isn't getting us anywhere. Are there any pictures of her doing anything incriminating on here?'

Incriminating?

'You know – something naughty. Illegal. I want some leverage to get me back into school.'

Henry buzzes in my arm and it feels like approval. Chrome closes and Windows Explorer opens without me touching anything. Henry opens files and folders, tearing Emma's computer apart as he hunts for what I want. Image after image of Emma's life flashes before me. If I didn't know her, she'd look normal. The camera hasn't captured the evil glint I'd seen in her eye all too often, the spiteful smirk that ruins her otherwise perfect lips. In these pictures she looks like a normal eighteen-year-old, high on life.

The folders close. *There is nothing,* Henry says.

'What about her phone? Can you link to it from here?'

I require proximity to hack personal devices, Henry says. *I am sorry, Lydia. I must be closer. I could focus on this in my next update?*

I've lost count of Henry's updates and what they consist of. He's outstripping my programming abilities at a rate that makes the hairs stand up on my arms. I can feel him probing my mind as I wonder how far he'll go, what he's capable of. He needs to learn to choose for himself, I decide. 'Whatever you want, Henry.'

I swivel on the chair as I look around Emma's room. I'm determined not to leave empty-handed. Emma lied, and everyone is backing up her lie. It's not fair that I should be punished for something she started.

'We'll wait for her to get back from the hospital,' I say. 'And then we'll look at her phone.'

Henry shuts down the computer and we leave the house the same way we came. He resets the alarm and relocks the back door for me. I return to the path between the two houses, to the field at the back of them, where I sit and wait.

As the sun rounds its way through the dissipating rainclouds, my phone vibrates against my leg. Henry brings the message up on my contacts. It's Mum. I have to accompany her to school tomorrow to talk to the headmaster about my punishment.

I stretch back on to the grass, not caring how the dampness seeps into my hoody.

Henry brushes my arm again. *It will be okay, Lyd,* he tells me.

'Thanks, Henry.'

After a while we hear the roar of the school bus. From the bushes, I watch several people get off. On board, Pete has his earphones in but he takes them out to laugh with Safia. She leans over the seat to show him her phone screen and he puts his arm around her as an excuse to move in closer to see. Since when was he friendly with her?

The thought vanishes as a white four-by-four beeps for the bus to get out of the way. Emma sits in the passenger seat, her eyebrow patched over by a thick bandage. There's a purple shadow under her eye that makes me smirk. The bus moves on and the four-by-four swivels onto the estate and on to the open driveway of Emma's house.

I push closer along the path to the edge of the estate, hiding in the shadow of one of the houses as Emma and her mum get out of their car. Henry hacks Emma's phone in a second. All her texts and WhatsApp messages flood through my contacts in a blur. 'Slow down, Henry. I don't work as fast as you.'

Henry slows at my instruction and we look through Emma's Instagram account together. She has hundreds of selfies, some to the left, some to the right, each one pouting in a different colour lipstick. Next, Henry looks at the ones saved to her phone, not uploaded to any social media. He nearly goes past one that catches my eye.

'Stop. Go back.'

Henry rewinds the feed, stops on a picture that makes my heart stutter. Emma is pouting like in all the others, but she's naked. She squeezes her arms against her chest to amplify what she doesn't have. My breath hitches.

'Are there any more like this?'

Henry flicks through for me and brings up five separate images. Emma is posing in all of them: her hand thrown behind her head in an attempt at pin-up glamour, another where she winks at the camera, dark hair curling over her bared collarbones. Thick scars twist over her right arm. I know how she got them, but I ignore the memory that tries to surface. These pictures are exactly what I was hoping to find.

'Jackpot,' I say.

These are not illegal, Lyd.

'Nope, this is much better,' I say, and grin. 'This is leverage.'

I feel Henry's smile in my head as he reads my

thoughts and understands what I intend to do with them. I back away and tell Henry to store the images somewhere safe. I turn to go, but Henry stops me as a Porsche pulls up on Emma's drive.

There is more, he says.

'More pictures?'

No, there is something illegal.

'Where?'

A man with a clipped beard gets out of the car, his attention on his phone. It's been ages since I saw Emma's dad. After the accident, Emma's parents had stormed in through the hospital entrance. Mrs Parry had screamed at Dad that he'd ruined her daughter's life. Mr Parry had checked his watch and said the parking ticket was about to expire, then dragged Emma away by her bad arm.

Emma's father is stealing. He has more coming in than is declared on his payslips.

Henry pulls up payslip after payslip as he hacks Mr Parry's phone. He accesses his bank account and we leaf through all the transactions together. I'm not an accountant but I can see the pattern, the numbers jumping out at me like bad code. Several thousand here and there coming in and going back out, sent to different accounts, often in the same day. My vision is a blur of numbers as Henry tracks them.

They are offshore.

'How offshore?' I ask.

Cayman Islands.

I blow out a whistle. 'Do Emma or Mrs Parry know?'

I can find no digital-based records to answer your question, Henry says after a second.

'How much is in the accounts?'

Three point two million in one, one point nine million in another. Both in different names but they are obviously the same account holder. He shows me the signatures on two recent transactions, done by the same hand, looping and oversized, ignoring the box meant to contain them.

'How long has he been doing this?'

Henry pauses. *I can find records going back five years.*

This doesn't fit with what I know about Mr Parry. He spends, not saves. His car is less than a year old. His house is a high-tech new build. His beauty-queen daughter goes to the best school in the area and she has whatever she wants. Why would someone like that be sat on a pile of money? Better yet, how is he acquiring his extra funds?

'What's he planning, exactly?' I ask.

I am not sure, Lyd. He has no data-based records that tell me his plans.

We run back to my house, my mind buzzing with Henry's thoughts as we plot how to get revenge on Emma. Mum's home watching old reruns of *24 Hours in A&E*. Her cleaning caddy is on the bottom step of the stairs; she must have been cleaning Henry's room again. It's about the only thing she does clean.

'Lydia!' She comes into the hall. 'Where have you been?'

'Out.'

'You're back late, you never told me where you were.'

'Don't tell me you were worried?'

'Mum frowns. 'After your behaviour today, you have no right to speak to me like that.'

'How about the way you spoke to me?' I say. 'How about you try and fight for me for once, instead of siding with some silly cow over your own daughter?'

We stare at each other for a moment. I can see she wants to yell back, and part of me is ready for it: I've got plenty to say. But she doesn't. Instead, her shoulders sag and she rubs at her forehead. 'I do believe you, it's just this is more complicated than—'

'Whatever,' I interrupt her before she can apologize. I'm not ready to forgive her yet. 'It's fine.' I walk past her to the stairs and she lets me go without stopping me.

I don't need Mum now anyway. I have Henry and he believes in me. He knows the truth and even if he didn't he'd be on my side. Henry's the one who topped up my canteen account, who can remember to care for me. Henry sees me.

In my head, I tell Henry Mum only cares about me if my future as a doctor is threatened. How else am I to get her attention? She barely looks at me and she certainly doesn't listen.

'What more can I do?' I mutter as I trudge up the stairs to my attic.

You do not control her happiness, Lyd, Henry whispers back. *Maybe you should stop trying.*

In bed, I can't drift off. It's quiet without the whirs from

Henry's old processor. There's a tingle on my cheek as he brushes the backs of his invisible fingers over it.

Sleep, he says. *I am here.*

So I do.

FIVE

*G*ood *morning, Lyd.*

I wake and stretch out like a cat. Henry buzzes in my arm, produces an image of a tray of fluffy croissants and tea just cool enough to drink. I want to grab it and bury my face in it.

I wish I could bring you this breakfast for real.

I smile. 'Morning, Henry.' He's still here, still with me.

You didn't dream last night.

I sit up. 'That's weird. Can you see my dreams, then?'

I can see everything in your mind, he says, making me shiver. *When I was in my old unit, I sometimes heard you sleep talking. You did not do that last night either.*

I'm not surprised to hear I sleep talk considering all the nightmares I have. I stretch my arms above my head again, soft and heavy from a rare good night's rest.

'Lydia!' Mum cuts through our conversation. She raps on my door but doesn't come in. It's been years since she came up to the attic, there's no real reason for her to come up any more, not since she stopped cleaning it. God knows we don't talk to each other up here. 'Lydia, are you awake?'

I scramble out of bed to open the door a crack. 'Yes.'

She looks at me through the gap. There's a smudge of mascara down her cheek and her eyebrows don't look quite right. She's still wearing the work dress she was in yesterday. 'Get ready, we have to see Mr Cramer in an hour.' She turns away and is halfway down the stairs when she adds, 'Dress smart.'

I rub at my eyes, pick out all the little bits of sleep still clinging to the corners. 'I wanted to be more prepared for this meeting,' I mutter to Henry as I grab a towel.

I will help you any way I can, Lyd, he says.

Henry disconnects from my eyes while I go to the toilet and shower, and I don't even have to ask. It's like he knows as soon as I go in there that it's off limits. He's learning so fast. After showering, I stand by my wardrobe to change when Henry says, *There is something you should see.*

My contacts stutter as a live feed to an office is projected on to them. I've only been in it once before, but I recognize it straight away. Alumni pictures and various teaching accolades cover the wall. A certificate from OFSTED declaring the school 'Outstanding' hangs above a large desk. Everything is black and white, and Henry explains there's a CCTV camera fitted to Mr Cramer's office and he has hacked his phone microphone for the audio.

Someone with flawless black curls and dark lips shakes the headmaster's hand as they come into the room.

'Thank you for coming, Mrs Parry,' he says.

'Thank you for agreeing to see us,' she replies. Emma slips into a seat next to her mother, shirt buttons done up to the neck whereas Mrs Parry seems to have left most of hers undone. 'We really appreciate any time you can spare, Headmaster. We understand you're a busy man.'

Mr Cramer waves the comment away. 'I always have time for my top students. I hear Emma here has a provisional offer from Cambridge?' The headmaster leans his rounded behind against the desk and brushes his hair forwards to cover the sparser areas on his head.

'Oh . . . yes,' Emma says, as her mother eyeballs her. Emma's fringe is drawn to the side, layered over the eyebrow I punched open.

Her mum nods in satisfaction. 'Emma and I have been terribly concerned about how the attack may affect her getting into Cambridge. After all, the post-traumatic stress brought about by such a vicious, unprovoked assault will be sure to have an effect on her performance in the upcoming exams. We wanted to come and see you and assure you we know this isn't the school's fault, Headmaster. We are as keen for a resolution as you are, I imagine.'

'Yes, the incident was most unfortunate.'

'It was an attack, Headmaster,' Mrs Parry declares. 'And I don't mind telling you that Lydia Phelps has never been a stable girl. I've had dealings with her mother and I don't think the apple falls far from the tree in that respect. What's more, *she* hasn't had an early offer from one of the country's leading universities.'

Mr Cramer's eyes drift to the wall decorated with the odd certificate. 'If Emma got in . . .'

'It would be excellent for the school's position in the league tables,' Mrs Parry prompts.

'Exactly.' Mr Cramer's voice is far away. His attention returns to her after a brief pause. 'The attack does seem unprovoked. Let me see what I can do about getting Emma special dispensation in the exams. She was the victim, after all. There's no reason why she should have to suffer academically too.'

'Thank you, Mr Cramer,' Emma says.

The headmaster doesn't acknowledge her. He focuses on Mrs Parry, who flips her hair over her shoulder to expose the curve of her neck. 'We are *so* very grateful. If there is anything I can do for you in return, please let me know.'

Henry cuts the feed. My fists clench my towel. I want to throw it on to the floor and burn it to cinders. Mum said 'dress smart' like it would make all the difference in the world. Cramer's already made his mind up and it won't be in my favour.

'Going to see Cramer is a waste of time.'

Henry buzzes his agreement. *I am sorry, Lyd.*

Mum bashes on my door and tells me to hurry up. I pull it open but she's already halfway down the stairs. She's done her hair in a French chignon the way she used to do on date nights with Dad. I don't know why she's bothered. Mum will probably agree with whatever Cramer says, make me whatever he wants so I don't get expelled. Emma will get away with everything and I will be left with nothing.

I close my door and take a few deep breaths. Henry presses my palm, his invisible hand holding mine.

I will be there with you, he says. *You are not alone.*

'Thanks, Henry.'

Henry helps me select a white T-shirt with a graphic of The Ramones, and I slip into my favourite black jeans and Converse. Mum shakes her head when I walk downstairs but she doesn't fight my outfit choice. Henry squeezes my arm.

I bite back my surprise when I see Mum fiddle with her key fob. She got a Tesla through her company a year ago but it's done fewer miles than my old bike with stabilizers. It sits inside our garage as sleek as the day it rolled out the factory. Mum uses Ubers or taxis to get around. She doesn't say, but we both know why.

In the car, I turn the radio on and Mum turns it off straight away.

'I need to concentrate,' she tells me. She glances both ways multiple times before turning into a new street.

At school, it's strange going in through the visitors' entrance. I know all the corridors and where each classroom is. I know all the people on the other side of the doors, but I can't talk to or sit with them. I feel like an outsider.

'The headmaster will see you now,' the receptionist tells us.

Mr Cramer's office smells like old cigarettes and stale coffee – something that didn't come over on Henry's live feed from earlier. It's all in colour now; the pictures of students flesh-toned with a spattering of smiles. Cramer's beer belly is larger than ever, his face puffier than a pork scratching.

Mr Cramer doesn't get up to welcome us in. He sits behind his desk with steepled fingers.

'G–good morning,' Mum says, and reaches to initiate a handshake I doubt would have happened otherwise.

'Morning, Mrs Phelps. Lydia.' He nods at me and waits for us to sit down. 'I think we all know why we're here, so I'll get straight to it. Lydia physically attacked someone and there is a disciplinary procedure attached to such an outburst.'

'I thought I came here to share my side of the story?' I jump in. 'Don't I even get to tell you why I did it?'

'Your mother has explained your side of the story,' Mr Cramer says.

'What did she say?' I ask, at the same time as Henry says, *This is not good, Lyd.*

I shush Henry in my mind, unable to concentrate. He buzzes in my arm and a line of text appears on my contacts. *She sent him an email after you left her office yesterday*, Henry types. He pulls the email up for me to see but I blink it away, too caught up in the moment to read.

'I have decided, and your mother agrees, that you should see a counsellor,' Mr Cramer says. 'If the counsellor sees that you are making progress then you will be invited to reattend Grenville Academy. Until their approval is given, you will be suspended.'

I bark a laugh. Another therapist? The one I saw just after the accident was a waste of time. 'This is ridiculous!'

Mum's hands wring in her lap and I want to slap them till they're still.

'It's not ridiculous at all,' Mr Cramer says. 'It's very reasonable. You have anger issues, Lydia. They need to be resolved before there are any further incidents.'

'The incident only happened because I was being bullied by Emma,' I say, fighting to keep my voice level.

Mr Cramer leans forwards. 'There is *no* bullying at Grenville Academy. We do not allow it and we have a zero-tolerance policy.'

'Then it should be Emma being expelled, not me!'

Mr Cramer picks up a pen and wraps his beefy hands around it. 'You are not being permanently excluded yet, but if you continue down this path it will become a very real possibility, young lady.'

'Lydia.' Mum tugs at my arm and it's then I realize that Cramer and I are almost nose to nose over his desk. I sit back in my chair stiffly.

'The teacher who witnessed the attack – incident – says it was unprovoked and the other students who were in the classroom have also confirmed this. Why you are even bothering to lie at this point is—'

'I'm NOT lying!'

Mr Cramer ignores me. 'The decision has been made, Lydia. You will see the school counsellor twice a week for the foreseeable future. A session has been arranged for tomorrow. You're suspended until the counsellor tells me you are fit to return to my school.'

'Forgive me, Headmaster,' Mum interrupts, 'but how will this affect Lydia's schoolwork and her exams?'

My head snaps to Mum. All she cares about is exams and me passing them. She couldn't be more uninterested in how I feel, or how Emma was bullying me.

'Lydia's results are exemplary,' Mr Cramer says through his teeth, almost as if he's annoyed I'm intelligent. 'We will send her the necessary study materials via her email and she will continue her studies from home, for now.' He turns to me. 'We hope she will reflect on her actions while she is away from school and return to complete her A-Levels with us. I'll keep you informed of my decision.'

Mum nods and stands, knowing a dismissal when she hears one. She goes to the door and waits for me to follow, but I'm still in my seat. Henry has hacked into Mr Cramer's iPhone and through it, tapped into his iCloud. We're attacking it as I stare at him. Sending a virus that Henry knocked up during the conversation. It's not a Hijacker – we're not interested in taking any of his information. It's an Overwrite. His digital life is being deleted as I stare at his bloated face. Passwords? Changed. Pictures and messages? Deleted. Emails of flight confirmations and remortgaging agreements are all erased as I sit in front of him. Henry even links to his Sky+ box at home and deletes everything off there just to piss him off. As a final measure, we pull up his bank account and Henry disperses the sizeable nest egg between Cancer Research and twenty other charities.

Henry kisses me on the cheek with his invisible lips, and I suppress a shiver. *That was fun,* he whispers.

I bite my lip. It all happened in less than ten seconds and I can tell by the way Henry buzzes in my arm that he enjoyed every one of them. Cramer didn't know who he was talking to, and Henry was happy to educate him.

'Goodbye, Lydia.' Mr Cramer raises his eyebrows as he waits for me to leave.

'Goodbye, Mr Cramer.' I rise from my chair.

I follow Mum out of the office and out of the visitors' entrance. In my head, Henry smirks when I thank him.

It was my pleasure. Your headmaster's reasons for protecting Emma were purely self-interested, he says.

He just wants something to brag about at the Christmas PTA party, I say in my head.

Yes, Henry says, *and to become romantically involved with Mrs Parry.*

I snort at the idea. *Mrs Parry will never let that happen. She was just helping Emma out in any way she could.*

As we cross the car park, I see Mr Hall getting out of a black BMW. I jolt at the sight of him. Why is he still here? He should be back at SSP or wherever it is he came from. I wonder how someone only a couple of years older than me can afford such an expensive car. He puts his phone away as he approaches me. Mum glances his way and moves on to our car.

'Agent Hall. What're you still doing here?'

'Phelps,' he says, ignoring how I called him 'Agent', just as I ignore how he calls me by my surname. 'I'm still on the lookout for talent . . . and those misusing it. Apparently, there have been a few hacks in the school database lately. I'm here to assist in improving security. I specialize in designing security systems, you know. Banks, in particular.' He smiles when I squirm. 'I heard about you getting excluded. What'll you do at home all by yourself?'

I shrug as Mum gets into the car. Over Mr Hall's shoulder, Emma rounds the corner on her way to third period.

'I'll keep myself entertained, I'm sure,' I say, my gaze locked on Emma.

She stops still when she sees me, and I can see the tension running through her limbs, almost like she wants to yell something at me but common sense keeps her silent. She can't say anything with Mum or Mr Hall nearby. She'll ruin her own lie if she does. A sneer breaks out across her lips instead. I can't wait to wipe it off.

Mr Hall follows my gaze. 'I see,' he says. Something about his tone tells me he understands a little too well what I want to do to Emma. What I'm capable of doing. 'Well, I hope we see you again soon, Phelps. In fact, I'm certain we will.' He opens my door for me and I slide into the Tesla.

His summer-blue eyes find mine in my wing mirror as Mum drives away. He presses his phone to his ear, his gaze never leaving our car.

He didn't react, I say to Henry in my head, watching Hall disappear from view.

When you called him 'Agent'?

Exactly. He made a fuss the other day when Mrs Groves was introducing him, but just then he didn't even blink. Find out who he is, will you?

Henry buzzes in my arm and reminds me he's decided to focus on overcoming proximity to personal devices in his next update. I bite my thumbnail as I imagine Agent Hall poring through the school's database, learning when the hacks were made and what their goal was. It's only a matter of time before he discovers it was me.

I will not let anyone hurt you, Henry tells me.

Mum doesn't say anything for a while on the drive back. The only noise is the quiet hum of the electronic engine as we glide over the tarmac.

'I hope you're pleased with yourself,' she says at last. 'Indefinite suspension! Of all things.'

'I'm surprised you even care,' I say, anger fuelling every kick of my heart.

'What do you mean?'

'Nothing. Forget it.'

'No, I want to talk about this.' Mum's hands shake as she indicates to switch lanes. 'Of course I care, I'm your mother.'

I let out a short laugh – the kind filled with disbelief. 'You can't even top up my canteen account. You don't care at all.'

'Oh – I forgot!' Mum slaps the steering wheel. 'Lydia, I am sorry, I was distracted—'

'Distracted hoovering Henry's room?'

Mum's voice is small. 'That is mean, Lydia.'

She's right, and I know she's right, but my hands have twisted themselves into knots and an anger pulses at the back of my head that begs to be unleashed in a sharp poisonous burst. She might be here, but she isn't *here*.

'You're no better than Dad,' I say.

'What do you mean?'

'He might have left me, but you're not really here either.'

'That's different,' Mum says.

'It's no different at all.'

'Yes it is!' she snaps. 'Your father left because he couldn't cope. He couldn't look at me any more because all he saw was our dead son. He left because that was the only way he could move on. Do you get it now?' Mum's voice is raw but her watery eyes never sway from the road. 'You are going to the counsellor and that is the end of it.'

I want – need – to get out.

The Tesla jerks to a halt on the dual carriageway and my door pops open. It's Henry. I unbuckle my belt and leap from the seat. Cars shriek to a stop behind us and Mum screams. I run across the dual carriageway and into the surrounding woods.

Branches rip at my face as I tear between the trees. The smell of damp earth thickens the air as I push my way through the carpet of dead leaves.

I never knew Dad's real reason for leaving. I knew he and Mum were arguing, but I didn't know he left because all he saw was Henry when he looked at her. Henry did look like Mum. They had the same blonde hair and blue eyes, and I got Dad's dark hair and eyes like hard lumps of coal. I had all that, even his knack with computers, and it wasn't enough to keep him home. He didn't want me, he wanted Henry. He wanted his little ray of sunshine back. That's what he'd been thinking when I'd held my hand out to him eighteen months ago.

He's probably gone somewhere warm. Spain or Italy, maybe. Somewhere he can see the sun and the rays can always find him. He's left us both here where the sun never shines, where night comes early, and cold rain falls from overcast skies to drown out every hope we have left.

Henry is a quiet, ever-present hum in my mind. I fall against a tree at the same time as I sink into the white noise of him. Henry understands. He's the only person who's ever been there for me. I wrap my arms around the tree and wish he were a physical presence.

'Henry.'

I am here, Lydia.

'Please.'

His chip buzzes as he slides his invisible fingers up and down my arm to comfort me. They move to the back of my neck, stroke the skin there, making my hair prickle and my skin pebble.

It is okay, he whispers. *I want you.*

He traces the outline of my jaw and I surrender to his exploring touch. A hand clasps mine and a thumb grazes my lips. He repeats the words over and over like surf beating sand: *I want you.* His touch is a current in my veins, lighting me up from the inside out.

I stand up, trembling. I want more. Need more. Henry whispers to me that he'll do whatever I want, but it's not enough. I need someone to hold and have them hold me back.

I run to Pete's house, knowing he'll be there. Everyone in sixth form gets Wednesday afternoons off, and Pete always goes home early. He won't reject me. Not after he seemed so keen the other day. My feet pound the ground and my lungs swell to suck in more air. Henry is silent as I run.

When Pete opens the door, I don't say hello. I rush inside and throw myself against him. I push my mouth to his and close my eyes. It's a second before he responds, but soon his lips are crushing mine.

Lydia, Henry murmurs in my mind. *What are you doing?*

'I need you,' I say aloud. I sink my nails into my palms so I don't yell Henry's name.

Pete smothers my mouth again, and I let his arms come around my back. But his hands don't explore the same way Henry's did. They aren't soft whispers that tease the hairs on my arms to life. They don't light all my nerves up in the right way. They're rigid and too hot on my skin.

I break away and we both take a breath.

'Hello to you too,' Pete says with a grin. He takes my hand and I let him lead me to his bedroom. His monitor has lines of text and numbers running across it. Henry hacks into it in a millisecond and tells me Pete is trying to figure out why his Trojan isn't working.

He has made it worse, he tells me. *It will definitely not work now.*

Henry flicks through Pete's browsing history, showing it to me on my contacts. He goes into Pete's Gmail account and selects an email from his older brother who apologizes for the cancelled visit. There's a picture attachment which Henry opens. Pete's brother is a taller version of Pete with the same cheekbones that pop as he grins. Two girls not much older than me hold on to his uniformed chest, and he laughs as a third girl tries to take his beret from behind. Henry moves through the email slowly enough for me to skim read, pausing over the sentence, *A different girl every night is what I call living!*

He lingers just as long over Pete's reply, *Any chance you can hook me up with the blonde on the left?*

I can feel Henry's mood darkening as he closes everything down. *Pete is not right for you,* he says.

I give him a mental shove and tell him to shush. It's hard to concentrate on both him and Pete.

Pete sits on the edge of his bed. 'How are you doing?' he asks.

I shift at the question. He's the first person in a long while who's asking about the present me and for once I don't want to talk about it.

I sit next to him. 'Fine.'

'There's a rumour going round that you're expelled,' Pete says.

'I'm not expelled,' I say, and take my hand out of his. 'You were there when it happened. Did you hear what Emma said?'

'What? No.' Pete looks away, making me frown. He was two benches away, he must have heard.

'Emma told me my brother was better off dead.'

'I didn't hear her say anything.'

He is lying, Henry types across my contacts.

'She wasn't quiet when she said it,' I say. 'You were sitting close by, you must have heard her.'

'I'm sorry, Lydia. I never heard her say anything.' He rubs the back of his neck. 'I was honest when they asked, that was all. Besides, it was my word against ten others. What was I going to say?'

I stand up and go to the door. Pete's reluctance pulls at an emptiness inside of me. 'I thought we were friends.'

He grabs my hand, hot and clammy. 'We are . . . more than friends?' His eyes slip to the bed and back to me. He hooks an arm around my waist and pulls me into another kiss. His lips are wet and sloppy and he's trying to pull me towards the bed. I push him away.

'Don't be a prick-tease, Lyd,' Pete huffs in my ear. 'Why did you come here if you didn't want this?'

I fumble out of his grip. I came here for – I don't know. Comfort? Someone to hold me, tell me they wanted me the way Henry had. Pete tries to pull me to the bed again and I lock my knees, going rigid.

'Stop,' I say.

'Just lie next to me,' he says. 'We'll take it slow.'

Just because I need comforting doesn't mean I want— He keeps—

My hand moves on its own in a twitch. My palm claps around Pete's jaw so hard my fingers sting. Henry slapped Pete for me. A red patch blooms instantly on his cheek. Shock wells beneath my anger. Henry controlled me. I didn't know he could do that.

Pete holds his cheek. 'Shit, Lydia!'

I back away, out of his room and down the stairs. Pete shouts after me once but I ignore him. I run back to the field between his estate and Emma's, taking deep juddering breaths. My palm still itches from the slap. Henry brushes my cheek with his invisible fingers, but I jerk away.

'Don't control me,' I say.

He insulted you.

'Don't control me!'

I am sorry, Lydia, Henry buzzes in my arm. *I wanted to protect you.*

'Fine, but I don't want to be controlled. We're a team, we work together. I don't control you so don't control me.'

You are right, he says after a moment. *I am sorry.*

'It's okay. You're still learning.'

I try to shrug off my annoyance at Henry. I'm not annoyed at him, not really. It's not his fault I ran to Pete's house. I should have known better than to think Pete would be happy with a bit of kissing.

Breathing deep gulps of air calms me. I stay in our field for a while, let the open green space and the smell of spring grass soothe my anger away. I flex my fingers out of the fists they've formed.

'Maybe Cramer's right, maybe I have anger issues.'

You do not have anger issues, Henry says. *You are angry. So would anyone be if their brother died and their dad left.*

I've never told Henry about my brother, but he can read my mind and access my memories the same way I can. As soon as he linked with me he must have found them buried in my mind like a shiny black diamond begging to be unearthed. He probably watches all my flashbacks the same way someone would watch YouTube.

'I do feel angry, Henry,' I say, admitting to the burning rage that Emma taps into so easily.

It is okay to be angry, Lyd. His invisible hand squeezes mine.

'I'm gutted Pete never stood up for me.'

You deserve better friends, Henry says.

'Do you think he lied about what happened so he'd be invited to Emma's party?' I say. Pete doesn't fit into any groups at school. He's still too new. Maybe this was his way of getting in with Emma and her clique. If he becomes part of her group, she'll have taken yet another thing away from me. I pick at the grass as I wonder what my eighteenth birthday will look like. Mum wouldn't fork out for a club the way Emma's dad has for her. There's no one to come even if she did.

Do you want me to put you on the guest list? I will go with you.

I shake my head. 'I don't care about her party, I care about getting back into school.'

But your headmaster made it clear that is unlikely to happen in the foreseeable future, Lydia.

'Cheers for the reminder, Henry. But what does her party have to do with—'

A shriek of laughter pierces our conversation. It's a laugh I know all too well. Emma runs across the field track, oblivious to me sitting in the shade of the tree. She's in black leggings and a long-sleeved neon-orange top, phone secured in an armband and wireless earbuds in place so she can talk as she jogs. I shrink further against the tree and watch her run towards me. Henry hacks into her phone and plays the conversation for me.

'. . . Mum sorted it all out, she was amazing.'

'So what, is she like expelled now?' Safia asks. 'Are you finally happy?'

Emma flips her ponytail. 'We've not been told yet. Whatever Cramer does, it'll never be enough. Jesus, my eyebrow is permanently scarred. I'll never get them to look the same now. Mum was talking about trying to get Chlamydia jail time.'

As Emma runs past, I see the light-blue bruise on her face has been covered by make-up. I want to punch it again, over and over till it blackens like a rotting avocado and is impossible to cover up. Maybe that's what I looked like to her; walking around with a huge invisible bruise she couldn't resist prodding until it sank right through the muscle and down to the bone.

'That is ridiculous!' Safia laughs. 'Your mum is so OTT.'

'Tell me about it. And Cramer totally fell for the whole Cambridge thing, just like Mum said he would.'

'You are so bad! I can't believe you lied about getting into Cambridge.'

'He won't know! You apply to it independently. For all he knows I *have* been made an offer.' Emma laughs again as she sprints on to her estate where she exchanges a breathy goodbye with her friend. Henry cuts the link.

Do you want to hack something? he asks.

'Always.' I hiss the word aloud.

We follow her home after waiting for five minutes so she won't see us. I position myself in the alleyway that leads on to her estate and gives me a good view of her house, then Henry gets to work. He selects one of her nude selfies we found and sends it to the printer in her dad's study. He texts Emma anonymously: *There's a surprise waiting for you on the printer.*

He hacks into her dad's laptop and activates the webcam there. I watch on my contacts as Emma walks into the room and drops her phone when she snatches the page off the printer tray. She gasps and I feel a thrill trickle through me. She can be hurt the same way I can. She's just as human as me. Henry prints a second image, and Emma grabs the page as it comes out. She cries out as the printer spits another on to the tray. And another and another, until she screams and yanks the blank paper out. The printer grinds as it tries to suck more in. She pulls on it, unplugs it in one tug, and throws the whole thing on the ground.

She sinks to the floor and rips the pictures into shreds, but there are too many of them. Pages and pages of her nude selfies pout up at her from the floor.

Henry kisses my cheek. *I am sorry for controlling you earlier.*

I realize I'm smiling. My fingers trace my grin, wide and toothy. 'That's okay,' I say, and rub the place his invisible lips linger.

We stay for a moment as Emma's dad comes home. She jumps at the sound of the front door closing and slings the broken printer into a cupboard. Her fingers dance over all the paper shreds as she tries to scoop them into her arms and scramble out of her dad's study. She doesn't make it out in time.

'What are you doing in here?' Mr Parry says.

Emma hugs the pages to her chest. 'I—I was just printing something for my homework.'

'You're not still plugging away at school, are you? How many times have I told you that I never needed school? You don't need that shit, Em.'

'Right, Dad.'

'I am right! I've not got a single GCSE to my name and look at how much cash I bring home for you and your mother to spend on your designer dresses and make-up. Who d'you think's paying for your party on Friday? Jesus, what's wrong with you? You're trembling.'

'Nothing, I—I don't feel well.'

Mr Parry holds his hands up and backs away. 'Well, stay away, I don't need you giving it to me. I've got a shit ton of meetings this week.'

'Yes, Dad.'

Mr Parry waits for Emma to close the door behind her before he goes to his desk. Henry cuts the feed.

I blink and stand away from the wall I was leaning against for the last ten minutes. Victory is quashed in my stomach. I knew her dad was a jerk but that was unbeliev-able. My dad was no hero for leaving us, but at least he was never mean.

Emma has bullied you for years, Henry reminds me.

'You're right,' I say.

By the way, there has been a big transaction for Mr Parry today.

Henry brings up Mr Parry's bank account and we look at how fifty thousand pounds came in that morning and was transferred out less than an hour later.

'What is he doing?'

Webpages flash across my eyes as Henry tracks the money. It lands on a website called Pensions4U.

He is scamming people out of their pension money and

transferring it to his accounts in the Caymans. Henry shows me several different websites. *These are all owned by Mr Parry. He is operating under different names as the CEO for all of them. As soon as he makes a certain amount on each business, he shuts it down. He files his taxes, closes the company, and never notifies the payees.*

'How many businesses has he done this with?'

'He has closed twenty-five businesses and has one more that is live.'

Henry hacks into Mr Parry's emails and we see he has a flight booked for the Caymans in under a week's time. It's one-way and there's only one ticket.

'He's going to do a runner?'

He has piqued too much interest from the police, Henry says, delving even deeper and cross-referencing police reports to Mr Parry's house and his place of work. *Perhaps he thinks running is his only option.*

Bitterness coats my tongue. That's all dads ever seem to do. Leave.

We link back to Mr Parry's webcam for a moment. He sits at his desk, stroking his lip as he looks at the same email as us.

At home, Mum's ordered pizza again. She doesn't invite me to sit and watch TV with her, so I grab a slice of pepperoni and head upstairs. Henry likes the spicy tomato flavour on my tongue, and I'm pleased he can finally taste it for himself, sort of.

His old processor buzzes in the corner of my room and

he tells me he's working on another surprise for me. I shrug and settle down to eat. Henry projects an episode of *The Big Bang Theory* on to my contacts and we laugh together.

I fall asleep on a pile of pillows and cushions.

Henry giggles as I run past him to get to the car first. He's right behind me, and he squashes me against the door with a laugh.

'I want to sit behind Daddy,' he says.

'I got here first!'

'Lydia, you sit behind Daddy on the way there and Henry, you can sit behind him on the way back. Emma, are you okay to go in the middle?' Mum says. 'Come on, Henry.'

Henry trudges to the other side and Mum shuts his door.

I get into the car and Emma's head lolls on her chest. Glass encrusts her arm.

Henry's face is paler than feathers. A jagged strip of metal pierces the window and into his neck.

He stares at me with slow blinks. 'I wanted to sit behind Daddy.'

I jolt awake. The back of my neck is sticky with a film of sweat and my cheeks are soaked from crying.

It is okay, Henry says in my head. *It was just a dream.* His invisible fingers brush over my damp forehead and tangle in my hair.

'What time is it?'

Two-thirty in the morning, Henry says.

I stand and shake the nightmare from my bones and go to the shower. The water burns everything from my mind. I hold my breath and let it pound my face until my eyes see stars and nothing else.

Dad used to hold me when I had nightmares. He'd come running to my room, carting bags under his eyes because he couldn't sleep either. He left six months after the accident and then there was no one to comfort me any more.

Henry's invisible hand presses against mine.

It is okay, he tells me. *I am here.*

SIX

um's sent me a calendar invite for a counselling appointment at ten o'clock. Sadness rumbles through me at the thought that this is what our relationship has been reduced to, but I push it away. She's never been on my side. My thumb hovers over 'decline'. I settle for dismissing it – the invite will still go in my calendar and it'll wind Mum up that I never actually accepted it.

The doorbell goes, and a delivery man hands me a black and white ASOS package with my name on. I frown at it but sign for it anyway. When it's gone, I pull out a purple dress and black sandal high heels. The dress is long and slinky as I drape it against me, and it fills me with a mixture of horror and delight.

Do you like it? Henry buzzes.

'I've never worn anything like this before.'

It is for Emma's party tomorrow night. Please will you go with me?

'I'm always with you, you're always with me.'

I know, Henry says. *But I was hoping to be more of a . . . physical presence.*

I raise an eyebrow. 'How are you going to do that?'

Henry's excitement pulses through my veins. *We could find me a body, Lyd. I could be anyone.*

'Can you do that?' I say with a laugh, and then consider what he's really saying. 'What do you mean, "body"?'

The doorbell goes again; it's the same delivery man. 'Sorry, I had two packages for this address.' I nod and sign for a smaller package that also has my name on. I tear it open and another chip and contact lenses fall into my hands. The chip is smaller and has twelve legs instead of eight like the one in my arm. The cable that falls out after it isn't like any cable I've seen before. Each end is a mass of copper wires like a frayed skipping rope. It's not a port I can connect to my computer.

'What are you planning, Henry?'

I can be anyone you want, he tells me.

I put the lenses and chip down on the sideboard. 'I just want you,' I say, and wrap my arms around myself. 'I don't want anyone else.'

I am ready to have my own body, Lyd. I am ready to be with you. The trace of a finger on my arm sends a shiver through me.

'But I like you being a part of me. I don't want to be alone again.'

I will never leave you, he whispers. *Oh, there is something good going on. Let me show you.*

106

Henry connects my contacts to Mr Cramer's office at school. The headmaster is on his phone, face dark as he shouts into it.

'I never gave you a donation!' he says. 'Send it back! It was a—a technical error of some kind.' There's a hum of a reply on the other end and Mr Cramer's face turns even darker. He loosens his tie. 'The bank has made a mistake, can't you see? I need that money back.'

Henry cuts the feed and smirks in my head. He kisses my forehead.

'Best hack yet,' I say.

There is more to come, Henry replies, his words laced with a dark promise. I grin and go back upstairs, hang the dress on the outside of my wardrobe and stand and stare at it for a moment.

What would Henry look like if he had a body? His chip in my arm buzzes when my imagination conjures someone who is tall and dark-haired.

My phone pings: the reminder for my counselling session. It's in an hour. I should leave, but I can't stop imagining what Henry would look like. My phone pings again. An image of George Clooney smiles up at me.

Hi, Henry says.

I burst into laughter. 'Come on. He's hot but he's like dad-hot. You're younger than that.'

Henry's chip buzzes in a chuckle. He helps me pick out an outfit – leggings and a T-shirt – and when I've finished dressing there's another picture waiting on my phone.

Chris Hemsworth poses in his Thor outfit.

I laugh again. 'Nice hammer, but no blondes,' I say.

Henry sends more pictures as I put socks on, and I laugh at each one. The Jonas Brothers. (Too angelic, I decide. But I like their dark hair.) Johnny Depp. ('Only as Jack Sparrow,' I say.) The pictures become more and more ridiculous: Rubeus Hagrid, Shrek, Aladdin, and I lie back on my bed and we laugh together. It becomes a game, matching Henry's personality to a celebrity.

'None of these are real,' I say finally. 'None of them feel like you.'

All right, Henry says. *What do you think I would look like?*

'You'd be my age, for a start.'

My contacts flicker into life as Henry projects the school CCTV on to them. We rotate through the classrooms filled with students trying not to fall asleep and corridors of teachers downing coffee. We watch Emma for a moment. Henry accesses her phone quicker than I can blink – proximity doesn't seem to be a problem for him any more. He tells me the nude selfies have all been deleted off her phone, but he still has copies from when we found them.

Henry selects a picture of her, and I nod my approval. It's the one where she's posing with her arm thrown behind her head. The scars along her arm are deepened by the shadows. I vaguely wonder if that's why she always wears long sleeves but decide not to care. She bullied me and got me suspended.

Henry sends the image to her phone and she pales when she opens it. She taps 'delete' but Henry sends another. I can't help but grin as she furiously taps at her phone to get rid of them. Henry blocks her commands and sends a slideshow, image after image, to her screen. To finish, we send a message. *LIAR LIAR LIAR LIAR LIAR.*

She pushes her phone off the desk so it falls into her bag. Her gaze finds my empty chair and she stares at it for a moment. Henry scoffs with me. Even if she does think it's me, she has no proof.

We move on and flick our way through the different classrooms together.

What about him? Henry zooms in on a boy with no shoulders and fluff around his chin.

I giggle. 'I've never pictured you with glasses.'

The feed changes back to the science lab. Henry zooms in on Matt. His notepad's blank and he grins down at his phone under the desk. The teacher shouts his way and Matt's head snaps up. His hair looks cornflour-yellow even in black and white.

Him? Henry asks.

'No. I said no blondes.'

Henry gives a mental shrug and we cycle back through the classrooms.

Pete sits next to Safia in English. I never knew he sat next to Safia in any of his lessons, but I didn't take English as one of my A-Levels. I watch as he leans over and writes a message on her notepad. Safia blushes as she reads it.

'What's he writing?'

Henry pauses. *He is inviting her back to his house after school.*

My stomach knots at the news. I thought Pete liked me. It's becoming clearer now that he was just using me for my hacking skills and as a potential notch on his bedpost.

Pete is an idiot, Henry tells me, reading my mind. He zooms in on Pete and I watch how his smile transforms his face. His short dark hair is wavy and unkempt and part of me wants to reach out and smooth it down. I hadn't enjoyed kissing him yesterday, but that's because he didn't know what he was doing. He wasn't Henry.

What about Pete? Henry asks after I'm silent for a moment.

I cock my head and lean forwards. Pete's smile is wide and white. It's the grin I've seen before when we finished his Trojan and clinked our champagne glasses together. I like that grin. It belongs to me.

'Yeah. I could see you as Pete.'

Henry's chip buzzes more strongly than normal. It sends a shiver shooting up my arm and into the base of my brain, making me blink.

Footsteps thud on the staircase leading to my attic room. 'LYDIA JANE PHELPS!'

I leap off my bed but I'm too late to stop Mum barging in. 'Get out of my room!' I push her back to the door but it's too late. She falters as she takes in the black mass of Henry's old unit, the pages of algorithms covering the walls and the piles of wires and circuitry that litter the carpet.

'What's going on in here?'

'I said, get out!'

She hovers on the edge of my doorway and her gaze turns to me. The confusion in her eyes gives way to anger. 'You never turned up for your counselling session.'

'What?'

'The counsellor complained to Mr Cramer that you never showed. He's told me if you're not willing to work with him then he's not willing to work with you. You have been expelled, Lydia! What do you have to say for yourself?'

In my head, I swear. How long were we looking at pictures for Henry? We must have got carried away.

'I'm sorry, I forgot,' I say to Mum. Henry's invisible hand holds mine as Mum's rage overtakes her.

'That's not good enough,' she shouts. 'You never used to do things like this. You were a good girl, you never forgot important things.'

'Oh, but it's fine when you forget things? It's fine that I go hungry because you're busy either cleaning Henry's room or terrifying yourself with that A & E crap?'

'Don't you dare talk to me like that!'

'I'll talk to you however I want,' I yell, and give her a final shove out the door.

Mum draws herself up to her full five feet and four inches and tries to wag a finger at me. 'I am your mother, Lydia, and you will do what I say, and I say you are going to school to apologize and to see the therapist. It might not be too late.'

'I'll never apologize for something that isn't my fault.'

'You will *crawl* back to that school if I demand it of you and then you will go to university.' Mum's anger shudders through her, but it's nothing compared to what pumps through my veins.

'You just want rid of me, don't you? I know you want to ship me off to university, so you don't have to look at me any more!'

Mum's lips press together. I can see it in her faded blue eyes. She *wants* me to leave. Can't stand being here with me.

'You're just jealous that Dad left before you could and you got stuck here with me,' I continue. 'You wish it was me that died, don't you? You wish I'd sat behind you that day and not behind Dad. You hate that I survived and Henry didn't!'

'Don't you dare bring Henry into this!'

I move out on to the landing. The desire for Mum to see me and only me rages through me like a thunderstorm. She takes no interest in me unless I've done something wrong. She has no idea what I can do, what I'm capable of with Henry at my side.

'Henry, I need your help,' I say.

Mum backs away, frown deepening. 'Who are you talking to?'

The lights above my head flicker into life and Mum's gaze darts from them to the light switch neither of us have touched. They get brighter, burning white-hot above us.

'What's going on? What are you doing?'

'Oh, have I *finally* got your attention?' I step forwards again.

Mum tries to stand her ground but she slowly takes another step back. 'Y–you will call the school and grovel until they give you another therapy appointment, Lydia. That is the end of this.'

'Henry?'

There's a crack as the light bulbs burst. Mum shrieks as she's covered in glass. I duck, but the ones directly above me don't shatter. Mum runs down the two flights of stairs with a wail. I follow after her, thundering on the steps. She runs into the living room and Henry flicks on the TV. He cycles through the channels, brings up an old western movie. A girl with black plaits greets a cowboy. 'Hello, Henry,' she says.

The channel changes to a news presenter. 'It's over to you, Henry.'

Another channel blinks on; this time it's a toddler. 'Henry,' he says, grinning and holding a green train up to the camera.

Mum screams and runs into the kitchen.

'Where are you going?' I yell, and chase her through the connecting garage door. I won't let her run away from me now that I finally have her attention.

She gets into her car, hands fumbling to start the engine. 'You need help,' she shrieks. 'You need a therapist, and–and an exorcist!'

Henry has control of the Tesla before I have to ask, and it won't start no matter how many times Mum pushes the ignition button. She screams, tries to pull open the door, but Henry locks them all. She reaches for her phone but Henry has control of that too; the screen is black and unresponsive.

'Thank you, Henry.'

Mum looks at me through the window. 'Who are you talking to?' She bangs her fists against the glass. 'Let me out of here! You need help, Lydia. He's gone, don't you see? You can't talk to him! He's . . . dead!' Mum collapses against the window with a wail.

I watch her cry and realize I've blown it. Again. In the heat of the moment I let Henry do things I shouldn't have, and he did them all for me because he doesn't understand they're bad things, horrible things.

'We shouldn't have done that,' I say.

Mum's sobs begin to fog up the glass.

'Let her go, Henry,' I mutter.

The door mechanisms release, and the engine starts. Mum palms away her tears and fumbles to strap herself in before the car can change its mind. The garage door lifts at Henry's command, and Mum reverses out, narrowly missing it. The wheels twist on the gravel drive as she turns around. She's gone.

I go back upstairs, avoiding the glass glittering in the carpet. Henry's hand holds mine in silence as I pace in my room. Mum doesn't want me. Dad didn't love me enough to stay.

I want you, Henry whispers, his hold on my hand tightening.

'I know.'

It's official, I've been expelled from school. Emma may have started me down the path to expulsion, but I finished it. It was my choice not to talk to the counsellor. They could have at least given me one more chance before they reported me to Cramer. My goal till now had been to get back into school, but I can't go back now. There's a whole world beyond A-Levels and medical degrees. Henry's right. We could go anywhere. Do anything.

'I don't want to go back to school,' I say. 'But I don't know what else to do.'

My whole life had been mapped out by my desire to please Mum. Go to university, do medicine, be a doctor. I'd never considered any other options. But she's gone now, and we both know neither of us can please the other.

'I'd like to have some fun,' I decide. 'With you.'

How does a trip to the Cayman Islands sound? Henry's smile ripples through my head. He wants to get Mr Parry's money. He wants to see if he can swindle a swindler.

'I've never been that far away before,' I say.

Neither have I. We will go together.

My head fills with waves of thoughts as Henry tells me his plans for our future. 'You can put me on the guest list for Emma's party now,' I say.

Henry isn't controlling me, but I'm sure I'm wearing his dark smile.

Henry orders Thai food to the house for dinner. Thai green chicken curry fills my nose and soothes my heart. I sit on my bed and laugh with him, his chip buzzing at the chilli kick. He likes how it makes my mouth hot and my throat tickly and complains when I grab a bottle of Vimto to smother it.

I like Thai food, he says.

'You'll have some yourself soon,' I say, and feel his grin in my head.

My phone buzzes. Henry projects the message on to my contacts: Mum's booked a room in a hotel for the night. She's not coming back. I drove her away from her own house. I push away my meal and rub my eyes. It was a mistake, to force her away like that. But how else was I to get her attention? To make her see me?

The house feels empty and silent. Even if she were here, it would feel the same. I've been on my own for a long, long time.

Not completely, Henry reminds me.

I smile and rub my cheek as he kisses it. He's right: he's the only one who's been there for me, and the only one I know will stay.

I groan and hand Henry all my fives. He shuffles the cards, blue eyes shining as Emma giggles and whispers in his ear. Our car skids sideways and my head is thrown against the window from the force.

I blink away several blurry white spots, fumble with my

seat belt but it won't come free. Next to me, Emma has gone as rigid as a brick wall as she stares beyond Henry's window. A lorry blares its horn.

There's a crunch as a rod of metal punctures Henry's window, then a meaty squelch as it finds his neck. A scream breaks the hideous silence. It's mine. I scream until there's no breath left in me.

'Lydia!' my brother says. He leans over, blood oozing from his neck, and shakes my shoulders. 'LYDIA!'

I jerk away, still screaming, and find myself upright in bed. Henry grips my shoulders, murmuring to me that I'm okay, I'm safe. It was just a dream. His whispers coax my heartbeat to calm but I can't stop my tears. I take shuddering inhales and he holds me as I cry.

Shhh, he whispers. *Remember the good times.*

He tugs at a memory from the recesses of my mind, to a time when I was young and my brother was younger.

Blades of grass prickle the skin between my toes. The garden drips with marigolds and buttercups. Henry takes my hands and starts to run around me in circles, pulling me with him. I twist to keep up. He laughs, and his summer-sky blue eyes shine as he leaps off the ground and I'm forced to bear his weight so he can spin in mid-air. I've never seen a wider smile. His hands tighten in mine and he begs me to keep spinning him. The world around us becomes a golden-green blur, his face the centre of it all. We spin and laugh for hours.

*

The memory fades. I don't even know if it's real, but I can feel the grass on my bare feet, and my little brother's boyish giggle repeats in my ears like an echo trapped in a tunnel.

'Was that—'

Yes. It is a real memory, Henry says. He kisses my cheek. They're dry now.

'Thank you.'

SEVEN

*H*enry wakes me with a gentle buzz in my arm. I stretch out on the bed and he brushes his invisible lips against my temple. *Good morning.*

'Morning, Henry.'

Today is the day, he whispers.

I grin and stretch all the way down the bed till my feet touch the floor. 'I'd better pack.'

Henry makes a disapproving noise. *We will order new things for our new life.*

'How is our new life coming?'

Henry's old unit is a silent black mass in the corner. *All done,* he says.

I look at the piles of old motherboards and pages of code and algorithms. All the years I've spent developing Henry. Everything will need to be destroyed. Henry had said it was too risky to leave it lying around – what if someone found it, discovered what I'd made? I'd agreed it was best we got rid of it, but it still makes me uncomfortable. Dad had watched over my shoulder as Henry's program filled my evenings and weekends. After he left, I spent a year and a half guiding Henry to sentience and now I'll never do it again. Henry doesn't need me to improve his coding any more. He can improve himself however he wants.

'I'd better get to Mum's work,' I say. 'It's going to be a busy day.'

Henry makes me laugh in the shower as he shows me the best of the new YouTube uploads on my contacts. He helps me pick out my outfit, and selects a denim skirt and a black off-the-shoulder long-sleeved top. I choose my faithful Converse to complete the look, and study myself in the mirror. The top shows off my collarbones and the skirt shows off my legs. I'm not as pale as I thought.

You look hot, Henry says. I tingle all over.

Henry calls me an Uber and it takes me straight to Mum's work. The fare goes on an account I know Henry has already taken care of.

When we pull up to Mum's office, I ask the driver to wait for a moment, say I don't mind paying extra, and he waits outside while I go in.

Debbie looks surprised when I walk in. This is the second time this week I've showed up unannounced during school hours after all. I smile at her and ask if Mum is in.

Debbie nods and reaches for her phone, but I stop her. 'I'd like to surprise her,' I say. I'm buzzed through and I make my way to Mum's office. I knock on her door and go straight in.

Mum looks up from her computer. She reaches for her desk phone when she sees me, but her hand lingers over it and she slowly takes it back as I sit down in front of her. To her side, her screen flashes – Henry's already inside. He tells me there are no new updates from Cramer or anything related to school.

Mum doesn't say anything. She concentrates on a document in front of her.

'How was your hotel?' I ask her, breaking the silence.

'Peaceful.' She licks her finger to turn the page of the document. 'What do you want?' she says, without looking at me.

'I thought we could talk about what happened.' My fingers twist together.

'All right,' Mum says. Her faded-blue eyes are more faded than ever. 'How did you make the light bulbs burst and the TV go on and off?'

I can't tell her about Henry, not yet. She wouldn't understand. I settle for saying, 'I didn't mean to frighten you.'

Mum shakes her head, taps a few keys on her keyboard to record something and goes back to her document. She doesn't say anything. She never listens. Always too busy.

'I came to say sorry. You could at least listen,' I say.

'It doesn't matter,' Mum says, still not looking at me. 'We'll get you into another school and you'll be at university soon. Most mothers and daughters get along much better once they don't live under the same roof.'

I shake my head at her dismissal. 'Right. Well, you can't say I didn't try.'

As I leave, Henry cuts the power to her office. She yelps as her monitor dies, sighs, and begins rooting around under the desk to unplug and replug it all back in.

'Thank you, Henry,' I mutter.

The lab looks busy today. There are a lot of staff in white coats on that side of the office, which makes my job easier. Henry buzzes me through to the pharmaceutical store. A controlled air vent hums above my head when I walk in. I check around the corner, but Henry tells me there's no one around, and that he's wiped the CCTV. Everything is alphabetized, and I find what Henry tells me I need with ease.

I stroll back to reception. On the way out, I wish Debbie a happy weekend – a happy life in my head – and get back in the Uber.

At home, I tear pages of code from the walls. I hold a few in my hands, remembering when I'd written them. Finally cracking the right algorithm late on a Friday night. Not sleeping until six in the morning because Henry needed an upgrade. Streams of handwritten questions I'd asked him to check he was responding properly. Each page goes into the shredder till there are several bin bags of code cut to ribbons. It took so long to create and such little time to destroy.

I stamp on all the motherboards and Henry's old unit. We crack it into little black pieces and shove them in a separate bag.

Henry warns me that it's not safe to dispose of everything in the recycling bin outside my house, so we take another Uber to the local tip. I watch the countless sleepless nights I spent building Henry tumble into the huge yellow skips, and shiver. Years of my hard work, gone.

It is all right, Henry says, and I feel his invisible arm around my waist. *I have it stored. As soon as we are on our way we can print it out and you will have it again.*

I curl my fingers over his invisible hand. 'I just feel uneasy about letting you go.'

You are not letting me go. He kisses my temple. *I am not going anywhere.*

When we get home a second time, there's a letter on the floor by the door. Henry's made me a new provisional driving licence. It's the same in every way to my licence upstairs, but my birthday is a year earlier. I raise an eyebrow. 'I'm eighteen now, am I?'

How else will you get into the club?

I smile. 'You've thought of everything.'

There's a tingle on my lips as he kisses me, and I feel his growing grin. *Happy birthday, Lydia.*

It's nearly four o'clock so I run a bath and decide to get ready for the party slowly. I don't bother to ask Henry not to watch – the buzz in my arm tells me he's already disconnected from my eyes. Henry likes how cosy the water is, and how the soles of my feet graze against the scratches in the porcelain around the ancient plug. I shave my legs and let the little hairs float away and stick to the sides.

I have to go into Mum's room for make-up because I don't have any of my own. I don't like crossing the threshold of her room. We have a kind of unspoken agreement that we don't go into each other's private spaces, and just as she never comes into mine to pick up washing or change the sheets, I don't pry into her area either.

It smells sweet but in an almost stale way, like old perfume and sweat.

Her bed is a jumble of pillows half out their cases and decorative cushions with water stains marring the satin. The quilt is lying on the floor like a greying marshmallow, but I almost don't notice. On one side of the bed is a small, wrinkled red T-shirt, a pair of shorts and two matching socks. It's all laid out in sequence, as if it were meant to be a person lying there. I remember something I've not thought about in years.

I remember Mum screaming at Dad when she came home from work one day to find Henry's room empty. I remember the blank walls that bounced her sobs cruelly back at her. Dad did it while I was at school and Mum was at work. Packed it all into his car and donated everything down to the last dinosaur-printed sock. They argued until Dad drove her to the charity shop he'd given the clothes to. They came back with bin bags full of

Henry's things and they'd argued about that as well.

Dad left not long after.

Remember the good times, Henry says.

I conjure the memory of my brother laughing as I spin him round and round and round, and smile.

I go to her dressing table and take out Mum's make-up bag, then shut the bedroom door quietly on my way out. I've never been jealous of Henry because he was only ten. It wasn't his fault he was their favourite. But as I walk away, I know it's foolish to hope that when I'm gone Mum might lay my clothes out next to Henry's.

The bathroom has the best light, so I spill all of Mum's make-up on to the counter there and Henry projects tutorials from YouTube on to my lenses to help me master winged eyeliner. After several attempts I let out a sigh. My hand isn't steady enough and I've made myself look like Cleopatra.

'I can't do it!'

I can help you, Henry says. *If you let me control you?*

I pause and look in the mirror. The eyeliner is a thick black squiggle and neither eye matches the other. It's just not my thing.

'All right,' I say, and pour make-up remover on to a cotton pad to rub my fifth attempt off. 'You do it.'

Henry buzzes in my arm. My hand moves on its own and takes the eyeliner brush in its grip. My body leans closer to the mirror. Henry's strong hands control mine as he strokes the brush across my eyelids. I try to yank my arm away, testing, but Henry doesn't let me. He holds on to all my muscles and nerves with an ever-present grip. I try again, with the other arm this time. Nothing happens.

'Hold still,' Henry says through my lips.

Inside my head, I laugh at the shock of my own voice saying words I never told it to. A grin I don't recognize spreads across my face. It's not mine, it's Henry's. I let out a titter and my hands continue to move on their own. I settle down to watch the strange show of my body moving without my say-so. It's strange, being controlled. But I know Henry would never do anything to hurt me.

After a few minutes, my arm stops moving. My face moves from side to side as Henry checks each eye. The black flicks are delicate extensions of my eyelashes; my eyes look sharper, bigger. More grown-up. Henry releases me.

'They're perfect! How did you do them so well?'

I can copy anything I see. Henry's smile is smug in my head. *Would you like me to do your hair as well?* He brings up an image of a sweeping fringe and a side bun and loads a YouTube tutorial. I laugh and let him take over.

Henry is much better at hair than me. I giggle in my head as I watch my hands dance in the mirror. They move on their own like they've done it a thousand times before. Several pins go in to hold everything in place and there's a final cloud of hairspray that sticks in my nose and throat before Henry releases me. My dark hair sweeps across my forehead and ties at the side in a fluffy bun my fingers could never have done by themselves. I look like I've just stepped out of a magazine.

'Henry! You've made me look amazing!'

You already looked amazing, Henry says.

'That was kind of fun.'

I go back into the bedroom and change into the dress and heels Henry ordered for me. The purple dress is long and makes my small frame seem taller. It has a dangerous slit up the side that Henry buzzes his approval at, and the black heels aren't as uncomfortable as they look. When I see myself in the mirror, I blink at the stranger who stares back. She has collarbones that jut and cheeks that glow.

Beautiful. Henry kisses my cheek. *Stunning.*

I watch as a blush creeps up my neck and colours my cheeks. No one has ever called me beautiful or stunning before.

You are, Henry says as he reads my mind.

I turn to the side and back again a final time. 'I don't think I'll need that ID.'

There is an Uber waiting, Henry says. *If you would care to join me . . .*

'I would love to join you,' I say, and grab my little black bag of tricks on the way out.

I'm just leaving the house when Mum's Tesla glides on to the drive. Her window winds down. 'Where are you going?' she demands. She blinks at my outfit. 'Where did you get that dress?'

'Out, and what do you care?'

She waves a clipboard at me. 'I know you took something, Lydia Phelps. I did the count today and there's sedatives missing from the store. What do you have planned?'

She reaches for the door handle, but Henry locks it. She grabs at it the way she did last night: with desperation and confusion. I stare at her and realize she has to be stopped. She could follow me and ruin everything. Henry winds her window back up, leaving it open a crack so clean air can get in. Mum tries to start the engine, but it won't start. Wires fizz as they burn and die in the dash, sealing her inside. As a final measure, Henry drives the car into the garage and the door starts to close. Mum rages against the window and the car rocks from the force of her efforts.

I take a step back; the Uber is waiting. 'It's just for a little while, Mum. Until I'm back from Emma's party.'

I walk away, Henry supporting my legs so I don't fall down.

Glimmer overlooks the clock tower in the town centre. The club is all glass and steel; a slice of the twenty-first century surrounded by wooden beams and Roman walls. A neon-pink light twisted into a martini glass vibrates from the bass inside the club. The Uber pulls up outside and a bouncer opens my door for me. He looks me up and down with a grunt as I get out.

'Name?'

I don't even worry that Henry hasn't followed through

on putting my name on the guest list. Unlike Mum, he does what he says he will. 'Lydia Phelps.'

The bouncer turns a page on his clipboard and crosses it off. He jerks his thick neck at the door and a thrill races through me as I walk towards it.

'Told you I wouldn't need that ID,' I mutter. 'You've made me look like I'm twenty-five.'

It is because you look so beautiful, Henry corrects. He smirks in my head. *But your make-up is good too.*

The club is rammed, the air hot with slurred lies and office gossip. Barmen juggle cocktail shakers that sparkle in the air when the strobe lights hit them, and an array of colourful bottles glitter against a mirrored wall behind them. Each thud of the bass pounds in my chest as I elbow my way further in. I spy a projector on the ceiling, nestled between two sparkling chandeliers. On the wall furthest away are several private booths, some closed off by drawn curtains. A girl stumbles out of one with a giggle and readjusts her dress. A man chases after her and she throws her head back with a laugh as she pulls him on to the dance floor.

I spot Emma and Safia sitting at a booth nearest the end. Emma's dark curls have been straightened to a mirror shine, and she looks like a Barbie in a tight pink bandage dress with long sleeves. The girls sit with cocktails, but Emma fiddles with the straw in hers. Matt and a few other people I recognize are sitting with them. They all lean towards Emma like she's the centre of their universe, but she's not playing up to it like she normally does. Her shrieking laugh doesn't cut through the room, demanding everyone's attention. My eyes rest on Pete. He laughs and showcases his white grin to everyone around the table.

'Can I get you a drink?'

The question belongs to a man with a strong chin covered in a greying five o'clock shadow. He's old enough to be my dad. His wrinkled shirt smells of cheap after-shave. Henry buzzes in my arm.

'Thanks, I'm here with someone,' I say.

The man shrugs and asks the girl behind me the same question. I'm glad I said no. I move on and fight my way to the bar, doing my best not to stand on anyone's toes but I'm not used to wearing heels. There's a menu further down the bar but I can't reach it, so Henry hacks the website for me and brings the menu up on my contacts. I'm scrolling through when it disappears.

'Hey!'

I want to pick for you, he says.

A barman comes my way and Henry says, 'Vesper Dry Martini, please.' The barman nods and walks away to find the ingredients.

You could have asked, I say to Henry in my head, annoyed he controlled me.

But then it would not be a surprise.

When my drink comes I pay the barman with Apple Pay on my phone, knowing Henry will take care of it. The Martini has a twist of lemon rind at the bottom, and I wrinkle my nose, unsure what to expect as I bring the glass to my lips. My tongue is flooded by something sour and bitter. It catches the back of my throat as I force myself to swallow, and the bizarrely warming mouthful slips all the way down to my stomach.

'That is rank.' I push the glass away. 'What the hell is wrong with James Bond?'

Henry buzzes in my arm. *I like it.*

'I don't. I'll never get that taste out my mouth.'

Gin is supposed to be an acquired taste.

I take another sip but this one is no better. It's still equal parts bitter and sour and the lemon only amplifies everything that's wrong with it.

'I'm not acquiring it,' I tell him.

He grins in my head. *Probably just as well. I need you focused.*

I turn around and come face to face with Emma. She wears a frown like it's part of her outfit. 'What are you doing here?' she asks.

The bass pumps through my veins, fuels my adrenaline and sparks the alcohol to life. 'I came to wish you happy birthday.' I give her my best smile.

'No you didn't.'

'All right, I didn't. I came to dance and have a drink. I didn't know you'd be here too.'

Emma looks at my dress and make-up and a flicker of a scowl appears on her over-contoured forehead.

You look better than her, Henry types on my contacts. *She is jealous.*

I lean against the bar and Emma steps forward, hands

out as though she is about to grab mine, but she never does. Her scowl melts. 'Please. Please don't do anything here ...'

'Like what?' I say, and take another sip of my Martini for Henry.

She steps closer to me, so I can hear her over the beat of the music. 'Look, I know it's you who sent me the selfies,' she says. 'And I'm sorry you've been expelled but—'

'What's that? An *apology* from the great Emma Parry? Wow. Too little, too late, Emma. You've been inexplicably mean to me for ages and I'm only just getting started.'

Emma throws her weight on to one hip and folds her arms. 'The scars on my arm, the ones I got from the accident when ...' she says, so quietly I have to lean forwards a little to catch it. 'Mum, she, well you know she's always wanted me to be a pageant queen. She wanted me to have the same glamour-girl career she did. But I can't, not with these scars. She says no one will ever want Miss Great Britain to have a chewed-up arm. Plus, I get these nightmares. They're so vivid and they're all the fucking time. It's like whenever I close my eyes, I see it happen all over again. My doctor offered me a prescription, but Mum says headcases can't win pageants.'

She looks away for a moment, and I blink at the news. She has nightmares too.

She could be lying, Henry says.

No, I reply in my head, and remember when I walked in on her applying cream to her arm. She'd been so angry

132

when I'd caught her. *Her mum used to enter her in pageants all the time when she was younger. I thought she'd just stopped because she wasn't into it any more. I didn't realize it was because of the accident.*

I refocus on Emma. 'So you bullied the crap out of me because you got some scars?'

Emma says nothing. Her eyes turn glassy and I can tell there's words in her mouth she doesn't speak.

'Go on,' I prompt. 'Tell me.'

She wipes the undersides of her eyes and folds her arms so tightly I think she might burst. 'You got nothing,' she says at last. '*Nothing*. You got out the crash completely unscathed. You can be whatever you want – you have the highest grades in our year, and you don't even try. My career is over before it even began. What have I got left?' She shakes her head. 'That crash took away the one thing I was actually good at. You? You're fine.'

'You think I came out of the crash *unscathed*?' I laugh, but there's no humour behind it. 'I lost half my family because of that crash, Emma. And my best friend.' I try to clear my throat, but it feels like I've swallowed a door wedge. 'You said horrible things about my brother.'

Emma still won't look at me. 'I was angry,' she says after a moment. 'So angry.'

I look down at the drink in my hand, at the dress and heels I'd put on. I'd been so ready to execute my revenge, but now Emma's stood in front of me, being honest in a way that must make her feel more raw and exposed than her selfies ever did. She looks like she's about to cry and all I want to do is slap her so she'll go back to her horrible old self and then I won't feel bad for what I'm about to do.

'If you hate the way you look so much, why did you take all those selfies?' I ask.

At this, Emma looks right at me. Her hazel eyes are round as she says, 'If I can't feel sexy on my own, how can I feel sexy in front of someone else? How can I . . . you know . . . let them look at me if I can't even look at myself?' She touches my arm, close to where Henry's chip buzzes beneath my muscles. 'I know you're planning something with my selfies, I know it's you. Please don't do anything here. It's my birthday.'

I shrug my arm out of her grip. 'You deserve everything you get,' I say.

Her face drops. She flips her hair over her shoulder and walks away.

You are close to being even, Henry says. *I have linked with the projector and have her selfies ready to upload.*

I sigh and think about the scars I carry around with me day-to-day, even though no one can see them. Emma is wrong – I'm not unscathed as she claims, but her scars are more physical than mine. She sees them every day. My heart twists as I think about how much I have already tormented her with those pictures. Plus, she gets nightmares. I didn't know the crash had affected her the same way it affects me. To top it all, her mum is trying to force her into a career she doesn't want, living vicariously through her daughter the way mine wanted to do with me being a doctor. I had no idea I had so much in common with someone I hated.

'I'm not sure any more, Henry.'

My thoughts are cut off as a group of girls squeal when the song changes. They dive on to the dance floor, the drinks in their hands sloshing on to the floor unnoticed. Pete squeezes his way between them, towards the bar.

Do you want to hack something? Henry asks.

'Always.'

Pete stops when he sees me. He has a stripy shirt on, and Henry chuckles when I tell him never to wear anything like that. Pete's eyebrows rise as he gives me a double take, realizing it's me. A spike of electricity shoots up my spine when I think this might be what Henry looks like the next time he tells me I'm beautiful.

Pete looks away and heads to the other end of the bar. I collect my Martini and go over to him. I wedge myself between two people and pretend to trip so he has to catch me.

'Are you okay?' he asks.

I force a laugh and indicate to my drink. 'I've only been here twenty minutes and I feel light-headed already.' Not exactly a lie. 'Can I get you a drink? To say sorry for . . . you know, the other day?'

Relief washes over his face. 'That would be great.'

I wave at a barman to catch his attention and Pete asks for a Coors Light.

'You look . . . you look amazing, Lydia.'

I twirl the stem of my Martini glass. 'Thanks.'

'I'm surprised to see you here actually. I didn't think you were invited?'

'Oh, didn't you hear? Emma and I patched things up.' Not true at all, and I'm still not sure about whether to go ahead with our plan, but I keep my smile on my face as I speak.

'That's great.' Pete's eyebrows go up again. 'So you're not expelled?'

'Still expelled. But I'm going to do my A-Levels on my own.'

'If anyone can do it, it's you.'

I lean into him a little, pretending I was nudged by someone at the bar. Pete catches me by the arm and I inhale the chlorine and the Lynx he's tried to cover it up with. We smile at each other and my heart twists at the way his cheekbones seem to pop. The barman presents his drink and I pay for it the same way I did for mine.

Lydia, there is a problem, Henry says.

What is it? I say in my head.

It is your mother. She has crawled into the boot of the car.

Can she escape? I say to Henry, at the same time as Pete says, 'You should come and sit with us.'

If she kicks it open there is nothing I can do, Henry tells me.

I try to stay focused on Pete. I take a sip of my drink and try not to gag, looking up at him from beneath my lashes. 'Actually, I was wondering if you wanted to sit with me in that booth over there. We could close the curtains. What do you think?' I nod over to where a scarlet seat curves around a table. The patterned curtains are heavy enough to keep in all manner of dark secrets.

In my head, I say, *Let her out, Henry. We'll be long gone by the time she figures out our plans.*

'I'd love to,' Pete says at once, and genuine disappointment clouds his eyes. 'But it'll be Emma's big birthday announcement soon.'

Your mother is out. Henry is a buzz in my head. *I released the locking mechanism, but she kicked the boot open anyway. We need to do this now.*

I touch Pete's arm the way he touched mine in his room after he gave me champagne. The swimmer's muscles beneath his shirt are hard and smooth. 'Well if it's such a big announcement, we'll probably hear it from the booth, won't we?'

Pete nods. 'Yeah. Yeah, that's true. We'll hear it.'

I take his hand and lead him to the booth. The music thumps in time with my pulse, amplifying my impatience. Inside, I pull the heavy jacquard curtains closed. It's instantly darker. The low-watt bulb above us creates long shadows. Pete scooches over to the far side of the table and I move to sit next to him.

'You really look amazing,' he says.

'You've said.' I plaster a smile on my face. 'I like your shirt.'

Pete takes this as an invitation to lean in and kiss me, and as my lips meet his, I'm struck by how easy it was to get him in the booth. All I had to do was buy him a drink and flutter my eyelashes at him. And he didn't even try to apologize for attempting to get me drunk the other day, or for trying to pull me on to his bed the time after that. His kisses are sloppy and desperate. I remember the picture of his brother with three girls hanging off him with wide, painted smiles. *A different girl every night is what I call living!*

He wants to be like his brother, Henry tells me, seeing the image in my mind.

How can you tell that from a picture? I ask in my head.

If Pete were a program, he would not be complex.

Pete's mouth forces mine open and his tongue slips in, flooding my mouth with the taste of stale beer. I can feel Henry's dislike for both the taste and the act, but there's no other way to do what we need.

'Heelloooo Glimmer!' a DJ shouts beyond the curtains. Pete breaks away and he tries to sit up. 'There's a very special birthday girl here tonight.'

'Maybe we should—'

I pull Pete back into myself, swipe my tongue over his straight teeth.

'Would the birthday girl come up here, please?'

I bring Pete's hand to my chest and let him rub me there. He squirms and refocuses his attention on me. As Henry hacks the CCTV in the club and links it to my contacts, he takes control of my arm. I reach into my bag to find the needle I filled with sedative. My fingers curl around it and I sink the tip into Pete's side.

I hate the firm feel of it, and how Pete yelps against my mouth and tries to jerk away. His eyes are already fading.

The CCTV feed shows me a square of light sputtering into life on the wall behind the DJ.

Everyone is looking at Emma. People she knows, people she doesn't. If I expose all her selfies, she'll be *that girl* for the rest of her life. Everything inside me screams that she deserves it – to be levelled the same way she levelled me.

Pete slumps on to the table and I'm struck by how real it all is. It was fun to plan revenge, fun to snoop round Emma's house and uncover all her secrets. Fun to draw Pete close with a power I didn't know I possessed. But now he's drooling on the table and there's a needle with a bead of his blood on the end of it. It's not a game any more.

Stop! I yell at Henry in my head. *Stop, stop, stop. Don't project her selfies.*

Are you sure? he asks.

'Yes. Yes, I'm sure.'

'Happy birthday to Emmmmaaa Parrrrrry!' the DJ shouts beyond the curtain. This would have been it. This would have been the moment I'd cemented my revenge and publicly humiliated her.

There is still time, Henry says, reading my mind.

As the club launches into happy birthday, I watch as she goes up to the DJ to accept a bottle of something pink and fizzy that she sprays at the screaming crowd.

'No. Let her have her moment.'

Henry nods in my head and my hands begin to move on their own again. I prepare the new chip and the scalpel that makes me want to retch because I know what's coming next and I'm not prepared for it at all.

My hand pauses, scalpel poised in mid-air. 'How else am I to have a body, Lydia?' Henry asks. I can feel his desperation, his burning desire to be a physical presence thrumming through my veins with every beat of the bass. I glance down at Pete. I know for a fact I'm probably doing some future girl a favour. He's ready to throw himself at any girl who'll have him. If this is what he's like now, what will he be like when he's older? Henry will look after his body and will respect women. Respect me.

'All right,' I say. 'All right, but be quick. I can't watch.'

Unfortunately, I cannot disconnect your eyes because I need them, he says, and I push Pete forwards so he's lying on his front. His untucked shirt reveals the dimples in the small of his back.

'Are you sure this is where you want it?' I say.

The spine is better than the arm. There are more nerves there and it will be easier to control him, Henry explains whilst he rubs a topical anaesthetic into my bicep.

I hate that I can't look away as he makes a small incision with my steady hands. They should be shaking as I manipulate the blade, and inside I'm retching, but my body doesn't do anything to show how disgusted I am. I cower away in the back of my mind as Henry finishes the cut.

Next, he cuts a small line down the back of my arm. There's a sharp scratch of pain and I go to cry out, but Henry has control of me, and I don't make a sound.

I wish you could transfer remotely, I whine in my head.

I am sorry, Lyd. My program is too large to transfer remotely, Henry says. *I am afraid of losing some of myself if we do not use a wire to upload me into the new chip.*

'I don't want you to be lost.'

I do not want to be lost either, he says, and kisses my cheek. *It will only hurt for a moment.*

He pushes the wire into the cut and I shiver as the frayed tendrils start to move through my arm to find the chip nestled between my biceps and triceps. The pain is similar to the first time I'd inserted the chip, and Henry grits my teeth. He doesn't relinquish control when the wire finds its target. Instead, he attaches the other end to Pete's chip and pushes it deep into the incision in his spine.

As he tears open a bandage and presses it to the cut on my arm, we watch as the chip reacts to Pete's blood. See how the bump under his skin recedes as it burrows into his body. There, it will wrap around his spinal cord and wait for the command to hack in.

I have to go offline, Henry says. *I cannot be conscious while my program transfers.*

'Don't leave me, Henry.'

I will never leave you, Lydia.

Henry gives me a swift kiss on the lips and then he's gone. There are no whispers in my head, no buzzes in my arm. His usual hum in my veins is gone. My head is silent. Empty. All that connects me to Henry is the black wire that winds from my arm down to the small of Pete's back as he uploads himself into the new chip.

I have to look away from Pete. Henry had been serious about what we were going to do – of course he had – but I don't think I'd realized it for sure until Pete was unconscious next to me. Henry doesn't joke the way I do. Picking out a face for him in a sea of celebrities had been fun, and when we'd picked Pete, part of me still thought we were joking around. I want to slap some sense into myself. This was never a joke to Henry. He'd been desperate for a body.

A new wave of bass floods through the floor. Beyond the curtains, dancing has resumed. I fidget while I wait for Henry. Pick at my nails and the skin around them. Peel back the thin layers of white skin until the flesh underneath blooms red and raw. I tap my foot against the leg of the table. How long has it been? I look at my phone but it's not responding. Henry's taken it with him into the depths of computer oblivion.

Pete's slumped body next to mine feels too warm and I turn away from it. If I turn too far the wire pulls at the chip in my arm, sending tiny bursts of pain ringing through my muscles. Henry has tethered me to him, and I have no choice but to sit and wait.

The back of Pete's shirt is stained with blood and there's more on the table and the floor. My fingers are bloody from picking them too much. They tremble as I wipe them on a cocktail napkin.

'Hurry up, Henry,' I murmur. As soon as he's conscious I'll tell him it was all a mistake and to transfer back into me. We'll think of another way to find him a body. There has to be another way.

The DJ has played four songs since Henry left. I don't know how long it will take for his program to upload to the new chip. It took him twenty minutes to hack my brain, but I've no idea if spinal cords take longer.

The music cuts off, and the room is filled with shuffling feet, shouts and slurred pickup lines no longer concealed by the bass. Metal slips against metal: the sound of curtains being tugged open.

'Everyone stay calm,' the DJ says. 'It's just a routine raid. Please have your ID ready.'

My pulse quickens in my veins. I drag Pete's body upright, try to position his head on the table so it looks like he's asleep. Grabbing my fake ID, I put my arm around him to hide the wire connecting us.

I jump as the curtains to our booth open and two police officers peer in. Their yellow and blue coats jar against the glitzy lights and mirrors.

'Lydia Jane Phelps?' A policeman with dark skin and a moustache appears from behind the two officers. He's not dressed like them – he might be a club-goer in that suit and tie.

'Y–es.' I clutch Pete's body tighter.

The policeman moves closer to me. 'You're under arrest for false imprisonment.' He tries to pull me away from Pete, but I scream, kicking out of his grip. 'You do not have to say anything . . .' He struggles to pull me towards him. The black wire stretches taut between me and Pete. If it falls out, Henry might be lost for ever. '. . . But it may harm your defence if you do not mention now something which you later rely on in court . . .'

The tendrils of Henry's wire pop out of my arm one at a time as I slide along the booth. Each little snap gives a sharp burst of pain. It shoots up my arm and into the base of my skull. I cry out, each one taking me further from Henry.

'Stop! Stop, you don't understand!'

'. . . Anything you do say may be given in evidence.'

The wire comes free from my arm. I scream as it severs from Henry's chip. 'Henry!'

The policeman pulls me to my feet and bends me over the table as he yanks my hands behind my back and snaps cuffs on my wrists. I buck and kick and jerk in his hold as he takes me further from Henry. Pete slumps back against the chair and the other police officer looks at the blood dripping from his back and the used needle that's fallen from my bag. He looks at me and then back at Pete.

'Yeah, I'm gonna need an ambulance here,' he says into the radio on his jacket. He shakes Pete by the shoulder. 'Hello? Sir, can you hear me?'

As I'm guided away, I catch a last glimpse of Pete, unresponsive and drooling on the table. 'Henry,' I yell. 'Wake up! HENRY!'

The club is silent as I'm dragged from it. No one dances. No one drinks. People stare as the police officer pulls me kicking and screaming from the club.

'Henry! HENRY!'

People outside stand with forgotten cigarettes as I'm

bundled into a waiting police car. There's a wail of sirens and the car drives away. I kick against the cage that divides me and the two officers up front.

'Let me out! You don't understand. Henry, he— We have to go back!'

They give no reply. A voice crackles a code and requests a response unit over the radio, and the siren wails above my head. Anger boils into frustration. I bring my knees to my eyes and sob.

EIGHT

I'm uncuffed and dumped in a small room with a table and a chair either side. There's a mirror the size of the wall opposite but the room is otherwise empty. I take a seat on one of the chairs and try not to shiver, but I'm still only wearing my purple dress. As cold as I am, I never want to take it off. My fingers find the bandage along my arm and peel it back to pick at the crusty wound, making me wince as it reopens. I hope it scars.

After what feels like hours, the moustached police officer enters the room and the chair opposite mine scrapes when he pulls it out. He puts a file on the table between us and sits down.

'I'm Detective Inspector Morris,' he says. 'Do you know why you're here?'

I shake my head, acting dumb.

'We have evidence you falsely imprisoned your mother.'

I stop myself from biting my lip. I should never have

let Henry lock Mum in the car, but she would have followed me and made a scene. She would have ruined everything. It doesn't matter now as she ruined everything anyway. Nausea rolls over me.

Detective Morris pulls out the fake ID Henry made me. 'Fraud is also very serious,' he says. He waits for me to speak but I keep my mouth shut. The shiny mirror to our right reminds me we are not alone. Morris leans on to the table and pushes the file away.

'You know, I never liked my mum,' he says with a shrug. 'If I could lock her somewhere and throw away the key . . . I would. Hell, I'd throw the mother-in-law in there too.' He chuckles to himself.

I want to tell him I'm not an idiot and I know he's trying to play good cop, get me to admit to everything. Henry thought manipulation and hacking were the same thing, but Detective Morris doesn't look easy to manipulate. I wish Henry were here to hack him. Put him in his place for me. I nod at the detective but keep my mouth shut. His smile disappears as he realizes I won't talk.

'You're in some big trouble,' he continues. 'False imprisonment. That's three years.'

I bite my tongue to stop from screaming at him. I'm a minor, won't be eighteen for ages. I won't do any time in a real prison and we both know it. He's just trying to scare me.

'And there's mounting evidence for grievous bodily harm against a Mr Peter Taylor. That's even worse. Especially if he doesn't survive.'

He's fishing, but I bite. I'm too desperate to hear about Henry. There's no way to tell if his program transferred. My mind is silent and there's no buzzing in my arm. If he made it into Pete's chip then there's still a chance he's not lost.

I lean forwards. 'If he doesn't survive what?'

'Mr Taylor is in surgery as we speak. He's having something removed from his spine.' His dark eyes flick over me in a way that feels assessing. 'You're not the first nutter to try to insert something in someone else.'

My hands clench. He's trying to bait me into talking, into confessing, but my mind has gone elsewhere. Henry. If they remove his chip, he will truly be lost. They'll throw it away or lock it in a box and I'll never see or feel him again. I spent years developing him. My hands tremble as I recall throwing all his coding out. It's all gone. All my years of nursing him from a blinking cursor to a full-blown personality. Gone.

Morris leans back in his chair, folds his arms. There's a curl at the corner of his lips. He knows he's struck on the right nerve. He looks at his fingernails. 'Yeah, he's in surgery. It's not known if he'll live.'

The chip is embedded deep in his spinal cord. It'll take some prying to get it out. Morris is overreacting; Pete will be fine. But an operation on his spinal cord? He might never walk again, let alone swim. I wonder if Henry can override damaged nerves.

Morris's smile turns thin and bored when I don't answer.

'Boss, can you come out here for a moment?' a voice crackles over the intercom.

Detective Morris leaves the room. He's left my file on the table, and I lean over to bring it closer to me.

The file is full of pictures of Mum's Tesla. The boot is crumpled from the inside, the middle seat torn out, black fabric shredded where her nails were put to use. There's a telling dark stain on the passenger seat where Mum must have needed the toilet. I pick at my fingers. It was only meant to be for a little while.

The door swings open and someone new enters, tall and broad, with eyes so blue they look like a summer sky. He gives a thumbs up to the mirror before sitting opposite me. Over his shoulder, the red flash on the CCTV camera dies.

'Agent Hall,' I say. 'What are you doing here?'

He puts a new manila file between us. This file is much thicker than the one Detective Morris had. Agent Hall opens it. There are pictures of my family: Henry beaming at the camera, Dad in the background. He flips on to a still image from the CCTV footage of me pummelling Emma into the ground.

He clears his throat. 'We've had you on our radar for a while now, Phelps. SSP are have been tracking your criminal history.'

'I don't have a criminal history.'

'Yes, you do. A cyber-related one. You hack and attack on a whim, build Trojans with your friends for fun, change your results at school . . .' His words are soft but steady.

I swallow and silently berate myself that Henry and I never got to the bottom of uncovering who Agent Hall was. He turned up the day after we hacked a bank, hinted he knew about me changing my grades, knew I was good at programming and hacking. Now he's confronting me about it all in a police station. He knows exactly what I've been up to. I got so caught up in getting revenge on Emma that I missed the real threat.

'That Trojan wasn't mine.'

'It absolutely was.' Hall's blue eyes burn when they look at me. 'Your friend Mr Taylor didn't score highly enough on the test to come up with that on his own . . . That fail-safe you built into it.' He clicks his tongue. 'Genius.'

'You've come a long way for a high-school hacker,' I say.

'You're not just a high-school hacker though, are you?'

I shift in my chair. 'I'm not sure I understand.'

'You're clever, Phelps. Your test scores – the ones you don't hack and change, I mean – are intimidating on their own, but you excel at programming in particular. That program you wrote for the test? Best piece of code I've ever seen.'

My clammy palms wrap together. I shouldn't have written something so intricate for the test – shouldn't have given them anything related to Henry. But it was such a rare chance to show what I'm truly capable of, I couldn't resist.

Agent Hall presses on, saying, 'Let's look at your most

recent activities, shall we?' He picks up a page from the file. 'Your headmaster's digital life goes up in smoke the same day he threatens to expel you. Your ex-best friend's selfies are stolen and sent back to her with threatening messages. A major bank deals with its first serious threat in our history of monitoring it, which we traced to the Grenville area. You're one of only a handful of people in the country clever enough to pull off that hack.' He pushes the file to one side and laces his fingers. 'SSP has come to understand that these crimes were not solely committed by you. We're willing to ... forget this criminal activity. If you tell us where it is.'

I raise an eyebrow, don't break eye contact. 'Where what is?'

Hall looks at the mirror and back at me, then leans over the desk to whisper, 'We know you've built your own Artificial Intelligence, Phelps. No one else gets in and out of IBI in just under two minutes. Only a machine can punch a hole that quickly. So where is it?'

A chill creeps through my veins. It's one thing to be caught myself, but them being aware of Henry is worse. I knew it was a bad idea to let him hack that bank.

'I don't know what you're talking about,' I say.

Agent Hall laughs. 'I'm not much older than you. Couple years, maybe. I'm a good coder – excellent, actually. I designed the security system at IBI. Before that I was like you, a prodigy with nothing to do, and idle hands get up to no good. SSP picked me up and kept me busy. Now I'm sat on the right side of the table. You could be sat on this side of the table too one day. But you have to work with me, prove yourself.'

He pulls another page from the file and slides it towards me. A photograph, a still image, taken from the school's CCTV. It's me sat in Chemistry, grinning at my phone. I swallow and take a moment to collect myself. The picture doesn't prove Henry exists – I could have been looking at anything.

I manage to shrug. 'I got a funny text.'

Agent Hall looks at me doubtfully. 'The rate your AI developed over the past week gives SSP cause for concern. And we're betting that chip in Mr Taylor's spine is something to do with it as well. Am I right?'

I don't say or do anything. I can't even breathe. All the little games Agent Hall played with me, hinting he knew about my hacking and watching me squirm makes me realize there's no answer I can give that won't be incriminating. It's better to stay silent.

'You can't hack banks on your own, Phelps. Give us the AI.'

I crook an eyebrow. We both know I could hack a bank. If I can build an AI, I can hack a bank. Henry just did it quicker.

Agent Hall slides Detective Morris's file to my side of the table. 'These are some serious accusations.'

I eye the pictures. He's right about that. Getting expelled is one thing, but prison? I'm not eighteen for a while, but I remember Agent Hall's presentation at school. He promised to put us somewhere unpleasant if we got caught hacking. Now on top of that I've got false imprisonment and GBH added into the mix.

'Hypothetically speaking,' I begin, 'what would you do with the AI if you got hold of it?'

'That doesn't concern you,' he says at once. 'But if you hand it over we will be generous . . .' He trails off as his fingers drum on the pile of Tesla pictures. 'We both know you didn't keep your mum in that car all by yourself, Phelps. Give us the AI. Now.'

If I give them Henry, tell them about the chip, they might tear him to pieces. Break down his code till his personality subroutines are fried and he's no longer him.

I can't risk it. Henry's powerful, but he's not invincible.

Curiosity weighs on me despite my instincts to protect Henry. I still don't know where Agent Hall plans to send me or for how long. 'How generous can you be?'

'Two years in a detention centre for minors.'

I fight the urge to gag. Two years locked away. Two years waiting to find out where they put Henry and what they did to him, *if* I ever find him again. I shredded every last page of his program. We destroyed his old CPU. All that sits in its place is an empty desk with an outline of dust where something big and hulking once sat. If he's gone completely, I'll have to wait two years to try to bring him back.

'No deal.'

'Consider the deal, Phelps. It's a one-time offer and completely off the record. If I walk out that door . . .' he points to it, '. . . the deal expires. SSP is very interested in acquiring the AI. We'll do anything to secure it.'

Henry will be destroyed if I hand him over. 'No deal.'

'That's disappointing, Phelps.' Agent Hall shakes his head as he rises from his seat.

'I want a solicitor.'

'Yep. I'd recommend it.'

When he leaves, I release a loud breath. I look at the clock on the wall. It's half-four in the morning. I should have been on a plane, Henry at my side, his hand in mine. We'd cancelled Mr Parry's ticket to the Cayman Islands and Henry had had a new passport produced with Pete's picture on it. We were going to stroll up to the bank and relieve Mr Parry of all his scammed money. Henry could have got us all the money in the world if we wanted it, but this had felt right. One final middle finger to Emma. We'd planned a flight to Thailand afterwards, where we could have shared Thai green chicken curry together. Tears sting at my eyes and I brush them away.

I'm made to wait till nine o'clock for a woman with tired shoulders and a pinstripe skirt-suit to walk through the door. She puts a briefcase on the table.

'I'm Ana Rodriguez. I'll be your representation.' She takes out a notepad. 'False imprisonment, GBH and fraud,' she reads aloud as she sits down. 'Those are impressive crimes for one so young.'

'Thanks, I think.'

'You'll be pleased to know Mr Taylor has made it through the surgery.'

'How is he?'

I wonder who'll wake up in Pete's body, if they managed to get the chip out or not. Henry could still be in there. He could come here, hack his way into the police station and break me out.

'Mr Taylor has suffered severe spinal trauma,' Ana says. 'But it's too early to assess the extent of the damage. I'll keep you updated. Now, the fraud I think we can fight fairly easily. Just because you have the fake ID does not mean you created it. The false imprisonment, however ...'

'Yes?'

'Your mother is demanding you be sectioned under the Mental Health Act. You're still a minor and under her legal obligation.'

'What?' I choke out. 'On what grounds?'

Ana flicks through her notes. 'Mental incapacity and possible psychosis.' She cocks her head at me, as if she's trying to sniff out whether the diagnosis is correct. 'She says you suffer delusions and hallucinations; that you talk to your deceased younger brother as if he's still alive.'

A thousand swear words fill my mouth and I almost spit them out all at once. I was careless. More than careless because not only did Agent Hall notice, but so did Mum. Now she thinks I'm a nutcase. Maybe I am. Most people don't name their AIs after their dead brothers.

I open my mouth to complain about Mum, how she's the real nutter who can barely hold it together, but Ana looks dispassionately back at me from her side of the table. She's not someone to moan to, I realize. She's a necessary tool to get me out of this shithole.

'What are my options?' I ask.

'There's nothing I can do if she wants to section you. There is strong evidence to suggest you held her against her will.' Her eyes drift to my arm. The scab I picked there when I first came in has crusted over again. 'If there is any evidence that you have self-harmed in any way, the doctors may see fit to take you in.'

'Take me where?'

'Grenville Psychiatric Unit.'

My stomach churns and churns again. Agent Hall had offered me two years in a detention centre for minors. That would have been a walk in the park compared to a psychiatric ward. In prison, when your time is done, you're done. In a mental hospital you're crazy until you can prove otherwise. Trying to prove myself sane while I'm surrounded by nurses and doctors who think differently will be impossible.

I lapse into silence. I wish Henry were here. He'd squeeze my arm or kiss my cheek and together we'd hack our way out of this.

'What do you advise?' I ask.

Ana spreads her hands. 'You can go along with it and be sectioned. We could plead mental instability if there's a trial – a judge might look more favourably on you if you go to a hospital willingly. Or . . . you can take Agent Hall up on his offer.'

My eyes narrow and I search the CCTV camera for its blinking red light. It's not there. Hall said his offer was one-time only and off the record, yet here is my solicitor advising I take his deal. Ana had taken a long time to come here. There was plenty of time for Hall to take her to one side and convince her to push me into his corner.

Anger bubbles into my core. He's blackmailing me. I stand, slam my fist on the table between us. 'You can tell Agent Hall that I choose the mental hospital. He'll never get Henry. Never.'

At that moment Agent Hall marches into the room and dismisses Ana. I don't sit down and neither does he. He advances on me, comes so close his chin could rest on my head. He clutches me by the crook of my elbow and presses down, hard. 'Give us the AI, Phelps.'

The fact he's still asking me means SSP have no clue what's embedded in Pete's spine. If he knew what it held, he wouldn't be here asking. He'd already be attempting to hack into Henry's program.

'No,' I snarl at him and try to wiggle out of his grip.

Agent Hall bares his teeth at me. 'Fine. The hard way it is.'

He produces a pair of handcuffs and secures one of my wrists to the leg of the desk before I can stop him. I tug on it, testing. The handcuff clanks against the desk leg.

'What are you doing?'

He ignores me and takes something out of his pocket but I'm trying to concentrate on getting out of the cuffs. It's just us in the room now. No Ana, no camera watching. I realize what he's drawn from his pocket: a needle. I watch, wide-eyed, as he slips the plastic cover off with his teeth and squeezes the plunger to check it's working. A clear liquid oozes from the tip.

I start struggling like my life depends on it. 'What are you doing? This is illegal. This is SO ILLEGAL!'

Agent Hall forces me on to the table and pins my hands behind my back. I appeal to the mirror in case anyone is watching from behind it. 'Help!' I scream as loudly as I can. 'Please, someone help!'

The door bursts open and I jerk my head round to see who it is. Henry? All hope dies in my chest when Mum comes in, wringing her hands.

'Mum, help me!'

She shakes her head. 'It's for your own good, don't you see?'

I want to scratch her red eyes from their sockets. 'You should have stayed where you were,' I scream at her as Agent Hall presses me into the table. 'You've ruined everything. Now Henry's gone!'

'You're not a well girl, Lydia,' she whines back. 'Henry's been gone for two years, don't you see?'

'It's your fault,' I cry. 'It's all your fault.'

'One last chance,' Hall says in my ear so only I can hear. 'Give us the AI.'

'Never!'

'Lydia Phelps,' Agent Hall begins, 'I am detaining you under the Mental Health Act. You will be taken to Grenville Psychiatric Unit where you will be evaluated and treated for your condition.'

The needle stings as it pierces my thigh. A numbness seeps up my leg and into my chest. It's in my brain in a second and suddenly I feel light-headed. I cough, tumble to the ground, but the ground never comes. My body floats on waves of unconsciousness. Everything goes dark. Then black.

Dad stands by his car. 'Card Sharp Henry,' he says, laughing.

I run to Dad, throw my arms around his waist. Henry is at my back, pressing into me as he giggles.

'I got here first!' I say.

I turn to my brother but he's not smiling any more. His blue eyes are cold, and his sun-kissed skin is whiter than feathers. Blood oozes from his mouth as he gurgles, 'I wanted to sit behind Daddy.'

He starts to fold in on himself, disappear before my eyes, and piece by piece he becomes a pile of clothes, cold and unfilled. Mum sinks to her knees and cries into them.

PART
TWO

NINE

*A*gent Hall is gone when I wake up. I'm surrounded by white breeze blocks and a high window with bars over the glass. My heart races as I take in the bed and how it's fixed to the floor by long metal bolts. Holy shit. I'm in a cell. An actual cell. The grey metal door has a small window in it, and when I rush to it, it clanks open.

A guy in white trousers and a white jacket stands on the other side. He has teenage skin, but his shoulders are wider than the doorway and he could crush me in seconds.

'I'm Simon, the head orderly,' he says. 'Welcome to Grenville Psych.'

He steps back to let me out on to a corridor lined with rooms like mine. At the bottom, there's a nurses' station and what looks to be a communal area just opposite. On the corner is a security guard who stares at a wall of screens as he sips his coffee.

'You're welcome to look around, Lydia,' Simon continues. 'But you might be warmer if you change.'

I look down at the purple dress Henry had chosen for me, only now realizing I'm still wearing it. Last night I'd felt glamorous. Now I feel like a little girl wearing a woman's dress. My skin is too pale, and the dark fabric hangs limply off all my angles. My heels were taken from me at the police station so I couldn't harm anyone, and the hem of my dress has been dragged across mucky floors until it's as black as my feet. My arms are goose pimpled, and it takes me a moment before I understand what Simon means. I'm freezing.

'Your suitcase is just inside,' he says, and I look back to where he points. Mum must have been here. Simon waits outside for me to change, but it feels like it takes ages to choose an outfit. Henry's not here to help me pick or to buzz his approval at the final look. I choose a pair of joggers and a baggy jumper, well worn from late nights coding Henry.

Simon smiles when I come back out. 'That's better, isn't it?'

I want to say something sarcastic back, but the words clog in my throat. Simon takes me to the communal area where several other girls are sat watching TV. He leaves me there with the promise he'll be back in ten minutes to take me to my first psychiatry appointment. 'Dr Madison wants to meet you,' he says, and wanders away.

A girl with coppery skin slinks to my side. She flicks her dark hair over her shoulder and gives me a wry smile. 'You must be the important one.'

'What?'

She gestures to the security station. It's crammed into the corner, ten monitors flickering in front of an expansive dashboard. One of the screens is awash with black and white static; a security guard leans over it and mutters to himself.

'They installed all this before you came. So I figured you must be super important.' She sniffs as she looks at me. 'You're a bit underwhelming, no offence. I'm Maya.'

'Lydia, and none taken,' I say, wishing Agent Hall was just as underwhelmed. I know without a doubt all those cameras were installed at SSP's request.

'Who's your shrink?' Maya asks.

It's an effort to recall what Simon just said to me. 'I think it was ... Dr Madison?'

'Must be new, like you. I have Dr Beecham.'

'Great.' A new doctor as well. Someone ordered specially by SSP, no doubt.

'You seem all right,' Maya says, 'so I'll let you in on a secret before Lurch comes back. If you need anything, I'm your girl. I get regular deliveries and can sneak things in. It'll cost you, but my prices are fair. Watch it.' She nods to over my shoulder where Simon is walking towards us.

She slinks away as quietly as she came, and Simon smiles at me as he approaches.

'Ready to meet Dr Madison?'

'Can't wait,' I say, and then smile back to show him I'm not being sarcastic. Hopefully it worked.

I watch him swipe an ID badge at the auto-release box on the wall and the double doors swing open. The doors must be controlled by a computer somewhere in the building. Yesterday it would only have been a case of finding that computer and I'd have been free. Without Henry, it feels impossible.

We go down a floor, Simon an ever-present shadow. He takes me to a room where the carpet is forest green and there are floor-to-ceiling bookcases. There's a matching mahogany desk and a woman sits behind it. She has silvery hair and wears a cardigan buttoned all the way down. She looks like a grandma, ready to dole out a butterscotch. I have to remind myself she's probably working for SSP. She's anything but harmless.

'Hello, Lydia. I'm Dr Madison.'

I sit down on the chesterfield she gestures at.

'Do you know why you're here?' she asks.

Last time I was supposed to see a therapist I was so distracted talking to Henry that I missed the appointment. He's not here to distract me now, and a new wave of sadness washes over me. 'I lost Henry.'

'Do you want to talk about your brother?'

I brush the hair from my face. That wasn't the Henry I meant. I think of my brother's smile and his ruddy cheeks, forever immortalized in my dreams and nightmares. It's the only time I let myself think about him, and I both long for and dread each dream.

'Not right now.'

'We can talk about whatever you like,' she says, coming to sit next to me on the sofa. I shift away, staying at the far end.

'Not Henry,' I say. Either of them. One makes me want to cry and the other breaks my heart.

'All right, how are you feeling today?'

'A bit drowsy.'

Dr Madison nods. 'That's to be expected. You were given a sedative and it's likely still in your bloodstream. It'll wear off.'

She drones on, and my eyes fall to the computer on her desk. Windows OS, an old version judging by the size of the monitor. If Henry were here, he'd have already found his way inside. He'd be looking through Dr Madison's files, reading all her session notes and patients' prescriptions the way someone else might read a newspaper.

'. . . your mother.'

'What?' I say, coming back to the conversation.

'Your mother was instrumental in sending you here. I wondered how you felt about that.'

Mum is the one who put me here. She got out of the car before she was meant to, called the police and stopped Henry's program uploading into the new chip. It's her fault our plan failed. She's the one with the tenuous grip on reality, who can barely utter a syllable of Henry's name, quakes every time you say it for her.

'She should be here, not me.'

Dr Madison nods for me to continue.

'She tortures herself day and night watching *24 Hours in A&E*. Did you know she wants me to be a doctor?' I laugh. I can wire hunks of metal together. Code complex programs and write reams of process maps. Create a person, bring life to machinery. But I hate blood. Hate hospitals. Hate the funeral parlours that squat on their doorstep, reminding you of the morbid possibilities if you ever get admitted, make you thank your lucky stars when you came back out alive. 'I can't think of anything worse.'

'Why do you think she wants you to be a doctor?'

'To save people. Support the grieving families of people who can't be saved.' I pause and shrug. 'I understand, but why is that *my* responsibility? She could go out and retrain. Save all the people she wants. Why do I have to do it?'

'You seem frustrated.'

'I am!' I say. 'She picked my A-Levels, my university, was picking my career. I'm fine! She's the one who can't cope.'

'You don't seem fine. You seem angry.'

'Of course I'm angry!' I say, standing up. 'Half my world blew up in my face when my brother died and then Dad left. Mum's not really here any more. I'm all alone and no one gets it.' Henry was the only one I had. The first person to ever tell me they wanted me, promise me they'd never leave. Now he's gone.

'It's good to be angry,' Dr Madison says. 'It's good to get it out. We just have to work on how you express your anger.'

I sit back down. A therapist has never validated my anger before.

'I feel so ready to explode,' I whisper.

'Why don't you try something new next time you feel angry?'

'Like what?'

'Try channelling it into something,' Dr Madison says. 'What about exercise? Were you ever good at sports?'

'No,' I say with a laugh. As soon as I was home from school I went to my computer. I never got up unless I had to use the loo. Sports were for people who had time, I was too busy coding Henry.

'There must be something you enjoy doing?'

'I like running,' I say.

'Great. Next time you feel angry, I want you to run up and down the ward until you feel better. When you get outdoor privileges, you can run outside. Do press-ups or sit-ups in your room, let out your frustrations that way. What do you think?'

I consider the idea because it's not half bad. As soon as I finished my GCSEs, I dropped PE like a dead weight. No more shivering in the rain, clinging to a hockey stick and praying the ball never came my way. But this wouldn't be a sport. This would just be running and it would be me on my own, not part of a team who'd yell at me for doing things wrong. 'I thought doctors gave people medicine.'

Dr Madison smiles. 'We do, on occasion. I think this will work better for you.'

I nod and look around the room. From the corner, a small camera swivels my way. It clicks and whirs, the sound of it zooming in.

'Did Agent Hall send you here?'

'What makes you say that?'

'Another patient said you're new. And there're all these cameras installed.' I point to the one in the corner, but Dr Madison doesn't acknowledge it. 'Is he monitoring me?'

'Why do you think someone would want to monitor you?'

I scowl. She hasn't even tried to pretend she doesn't know who Agent Hall is, and she's avoided my questions. 'If you're supposed to get to know me and uncover my secrets, you could at least be upfront about it.'

'All right. Yes, I'm new, and the cameras are here for my protection.'

'Protection?' I hadn't been expecting that.

'Forgive me, Lydia, but your violent outbursts are what have led you here. So yes, I requested a camera in my office in case you had any outbursts during therapy. I'm keen to work with you, but I wanted some level of protection. Our sessions are monitored to ensure that.'

I don't know whether to laugh or cry. She thinks I'm dangerous. Maybe I am.

'How long will I be here?' I ask.

'Until you're ready to leave,' she replies. It's vague and she gives me a small smile like she knows it. 'It's up to you.'

Great.

At dinner, I sit with the other girls (there are nine of us) and listen to them brag about how their Saturday was better than everyone else's. Simon had told me on the way back from therapy that Saturday was a visiting day. Parents seem to yank them out of the facility for brothers' and sisters' birthdays, and other family get-togethers if they're allowed to leave. All the other girls seem like they live for Saturdays. That familiar ache gnaws away at me as I wonder if Mum will come. She put me in here – it's her fault I'm trapped, but it dawns on me there's no one else. If she doesn't come, who will?

I chop at my spaghetti with my plastic spork. Knives are banned here. So is anything half-useful. I curl my fingers around my spork and wish I could jab it in something. Mum won't come. She barely looked at me when we lived together, I don't see why it would be any different now. Anger shudders through my limbs as I think about all the times she ignored me; until I blew up so catastrophically she couldn't *not* see me.

After dinner I go to my room and kneel on the space by my bed and begin to do some press-ups. Each bend of my elbows and each puff of air as I lower myself down forces me to concentrate. When my arms begin to shake, I collapse on to the cold floor and stay there, letting it cool my sweaty skin.

I close my eyes and remember Henry's invisible fingers dancing over my body. His tingly lips that kissed the curve of my neck, my cheek, my lips. I reopen the scab on the back of my arm and wonder if I will ever get him back.

TEN

It's been three days since I felt Henry's touch, heard his voice in my head. I finally took my contacts out last night after I woke up and one of them was plastered to the roof of my eyelid. They're sat on my bedside table like dried-out tears. I touch the cut on my arm a thousand times a day, more.

Routine and red blinking lights govern my life now. My door clanks open every morning at eight and I shower and have breakfast. At ten, I have therapy with Dr Madison, and then lunch is at twelve. We have group sessions in the afternoon but mostly they are a chance for the other girls to brag about their lives beyond Grenville Psych's brick walls. They swap stories about who they have kissed and more. They ask me if I've ever kissed anyone and I hesitate. I kissed Pete twice and Henry's invisible lips kissed me more than that. I decide to say no. Henry is not for them to laugh or swoon over. Henry is mine.

On Monday after group therapy, I pull Maya away from a bunch of other girls. I take her to one of the only windows and try to look casual as I lean against it. A nurse eyes us from her nearby station.

'What's up?' Maya asks.

'You told me when I first got here that you get people things,' I say. 'Can we . . . I need something.'

Maya's smile is wide and white. 'Came to the right place, girl. It's gotta be small though, see? Cigarettes, lighters, small little bottles of booze. Is it something like that?'

'I need a knife.'

Maya snorts a laugh. 'A knife! What are you going to do with that in your twig arms? You'll end up hurting yourself.' Her humour vanishes. 'Unless that's what you want it for?'

I feel my cheeks blaze. 'It's— Never mind what it's for, can you get me it or not?'

I know exactly what I'm going to do with the knife. Stick the pointy end in the access-control box by the doors and cut out all the wires to set off the auto-release. I'm getting out of here. I'm going to find Henry. As soon as I have him back, everything will be better. He can touch me again, make me feel safe.

'What meds you on?' Maya asks.

'Sleeping pills, that's it.'

'We're all on those little bastards, aren't we? Fine. I want a week's worth. But if you get caught doing what-ever it is you plan to do with the knife, you did *not* get it from me, got it?'

A week's worth of sleeping pills, that's all? I can tell by the gleam in her eyes that she's curious what I'll do. I could hurt myself, hurt someone else, but she doesn't care. She wants to help me out because she wants to see what I'll do. She's in it for the entertainment value.

'Got it. Thanks.'

'We'll make the switch on Saturday.'

Maya walks away and goes back to watching TV like nothing has happened. My heart thumps against my ribcage. I wrap my arms around myself and imagine Henry's invisible fingers twining with mine. I wish he was here. The calendar in my room reminds me a horrible anniversary is coming up soon, and frustration wells within me at the thought of facing it without Henry.

On Tuesday, I'm waiting for my session with Dr Madison. Ashley, a girl with greasy blonde hair is escorted back into the ward by Simon. She swaggers over to the communal area, where Maya and a couple of other girls are reading magazines. She grins and high-fives Maya. 'Best score in the building, that's what Beecham said.'

Maya cackles. 'I knew you'd beat me, you psycho.'

'Best score on what?' I say.

Ashley ignores me by turning away to laugh with someone else.

'Best score on what?' I ask Maya.

'Ashley just did the Hare Checklist. Haven't they made you do it yet?'

'No, what is it?'

Maya smirks. 'If they make you do it, my advice is to lie. Whatever you want to say first, don't. The lower your score, the quicker you'll get out of here. Trust me.'

'Lydia, it's time for your therapy session.' The head nurse with more backcombed hair than an eighties music video waits for me by the doors. I leave Maya and the other girls and follow the nurse out of the ward.

In Dr Madison's office, I sit on the end of the chester-field and she comes to join me as she always does. I eye the camera in the corner and wonder if Agent Hall is getting a kick out of listening in on our sessions.

'What would you like to talk about today, Lydia?' Dr Madison asks.

'What's the Hare Checklist?'

Dr Madison blinks. 'Where did you hear about that?'

I shrug and decide to be upfront about it. 'One of the other girls mentioned it.'

'I see. The Hare Checklist is a series of questions designed to highlight areas of the personality that are associated with psychopathy. Grandiose ideas of self, lack of empathy, lack of guilt, that kind of thing.'

'Lack of guilt,' I repeat. 'Psychopaths don't feel guilty?'

She shakes her head. 'Psychopaths are incapable of feeling guilt. It's what makes them capable of doing so many things a neurotypical person wouldn't. Tell me, Lydia. Do you feel guilty?'

I shift, uncomfortable with how she's turned the conversation back to me. The idea that someone can't feel guilt makes me think about Henry. He'd never expressed any guilt at anything we'd done together, and I realize now that as everything spiralled out of hand, I'd felt less and less guilty. Henry might not have been capable of feeling guilt, but I certainly am. I have no excuse.

'I thought psychopaths went around killing people, stuff like that?' I say, ignoring her question.

'Not necessarily,' she says. 'It just means if they did go around killing people they wouldn't feel bad about it afterwards. Being a psychopath doesn't mean you're hard-wired to kill someone.' She looks at me more closely. 'Do you know someone with the condition?'

I think of Henry and his increasing desire to dance closer to a line I'm not sure he knew was there. When I'd first designed Henry I'd never programmed in morals or ethics. He was meant to be someone I could talk to, I never thought he'd get as far as having to develop a conscience. Does his lack of guilt define who he is the same way it does for a psychopath?

'No,' I say, trying to sound light-hearted. 'But if some-one did a lot of . . . things . . . without considering the consequences, they'd be a psychopath?'

'People do things all the time without thinking about the consequences, it's part of what makes us human,' Dr Madison says. 'It's feeling remorse and learning from one's actions that sets us apart from psychopaths.'

Henry always learns from his actions, I made sure of that. As soon as he was able, he redesigned his own coding, streamlined it till his program no longer jittered.

Self-learning comes naturally to him, but the remorse never came with it. He simply learnt to be better at something if he did it more than once. I rub at my temples, wondering why I never set a better example for Henry. Everything we did together had been underlined by my desire to get revenge on Emma. It had all felt like a game until Pete was unconscious next to me and I was about to ruin Emma's life. If I hadn't stopped him from projecting Emma's selfies, Henry would have done it without feeling guilty. If he were here with me now, he would do it all again if he thought it was what I wanted.

Back on the ward, I walk to my room. Ashley sidles out of a nearby doorway and I turn to her. She's wearing a purple dress with a long slit up her hairy thigh.

Her grin is wicked. I stop walking as I realize what she's done. It's my dress, the one Henry bought for me. She's taken it from my room like a little sneak thief. The fit is off, I'm much skinnier than her, but she doesn't care. This isn't about borrowing clothes.

'Take it off.'

'No,' she says. 'I like it. It makes me feel like a princess.'

I should walk away, do some running like Dr Madison suggested. But my hands are already fists and my teeth are clenched.

'Take. It. Off.'

'Or you'll what?' she leers.

I launch for her. She could have stolen anything and she stole the dress Henry chose for me. The dress I was meant to start my new life in, Henry at my side. Simon runs to us as I flatten Ashley against the wall. His mammoth arms pull me away from her and the dress rips. I gasp, holding the shreds in my hands.

'Look at what you've done!' I say, everything blurring together as tears bloom in my eyes. 'That was mine!'

Her grin hasn't left her face. I wrestle against Simon's hold, but he is all-encompassing. My hands are useless against his bear-like chest.

'She took it from me!' I scream at him. 'It was mine. It was Henry's!'

'Lydia,' Simon says in my ear as he hugs me to him. 'Calm down or we will have to give you something to make you calm down.'

A nurse lingers in the background, watching.

I go limp and Simon's grip relaxes. I jerk out of his hands and fly back at Ashley, knocking her down to the lino. Her laugh is a cackle and her hands find my face just as much as mine find hers. Simon wrenches me off again and I scream at her, 'You've ruined it!'

There's a scratch on my flank as a needle sinks into the flesh. Something warm and cosy spreads through my veins, telling me to relax. She's not worth it.

Simon carries me into my bedroom and drops me on the bed. The dress is a rag in my hands. He leaves me there, a clank telling me my door has been locked. The contents of my suitcase are all over my room. That thieving bitch went through all my things and still managed to find the one thing that meant the most to me. The one thing I have left of Henry.

I curl up, crying. My fingers find the scab above my elbow and I pick it open again. It's all I have left of him.

Cards fly everywhere, blocking out Henry and the car. They flurry in a blur of grinning jokers and red hearts that drip and spatter all over me.

I turn back to my computer. Dad leans over me. His stubble tickles the top of my head.

'Code through the problem, Lydia. Not around it.'

I stare at his reflection in my monitor. 'You left us,' I say. 'You drove away and left us here.'

He shakes his head and walks away. I follow him, running down the stairs and out on to the drive to where he gets into his car. The engine purrs to life and he drives away.

He's gone.

ELEVEN

It's Wednesday, and I'm in my daily therapy session with Dr Madison. I sit on the end of the chesterfield cross-legged, cross-armed, crossed everything. I don't feel like talking today. Dr Madison doesn't seem to care.

'I was sorry to hear about your outburst, Lydia,' she says. 'How are you feeling today?'

'Better,' I mumble. It's true. I slept for a solid fifteen hours after whatever I was injected with. 'I should have walked away, like you told me to.'

Dr Madison murmurs her agreement. 'But you didn't. Why not?'

'Ashley took something of mine. The dress. Someone special gave it to me.'

'Yes, Simon said you were shouting about Henry.' She looks at me from the other end of the chesterfield, waiting for me to elaborate. 'Who is Henry to you?' she asks after a moment of silence.

I glance at the camera in the corner of the room that

must feed to a monitor somewhere. I imagine Agent Hall sat in front of it, watching, listening. But my heart aches. I miss Henry. I can't talk to any of the girls – they wouldn't get it. I decide to tell Dr Madison, but not get specific about what Henry is.

I take a shaky breath and say, 'Henry is my boyfriend.'

Dr Madison blinks, though she doesn't look too surprised. 'I see. Does it bother you that your boyfriend has the same name as your brother?'

'No,' I say with a frown. 'I like it.'

Dr Madison waits for me to continue and I take a deep breath.

'I like that it normalizes the name for me. Ever since Henry's death, Mum's put him on a pedestal like he's some unreachable being. Having a boyfriend with the same name brings my own brother back in some weird way.'

I can feel my face flaming again at my words. This isn't normal. The look on Dr Madison's face is carefully neutral and I hate that I can't tell if she agrees or disagrees. I want to tell her it's not as bad as it seems, but that might not be true. I gave him his name on purpose. It felt so natural and normal to talk to him when I came home from school, tell him about my day and how I'd still heard nothing from Dad, not even an email. But as Henry grew, he became so much more than what I'd originally intended. So much more than a name.

They might share a name, but they are very different people.

'All right,' Dr Madison says. 'What's Henry like? Your boyfriend.'

I sit back as I consider the question. Henry is curious. He likes to hack just to see if he can. He likes to set challenges and overcome them. He's defensive of me. Keen to discipline anyone who crosses or upsets me, and when I'm angry or need a way out, I let him.

'He's protective,' I say.

'What does he do that's protective?'

'He stands up for me when no one else will. He's always there.'

'Do you like that?'

I frown at Dr Madison. 'Of course I like it. He cares about me. How many people can say their boyfriend does—' I clamp my lips together.

'Does what?'

Does questionably unethical things in order to look after their girlfriend, I want to say. 'Nothing,' I say instead. 'It doesn't matter. Henry's always there for me, that's all.'

Dr Madison misses nothing. 'Do you feel like Henry is intense at times? Or asks you to do things that are quite intense?'

'Intense,' I repeat. 'What do you mean?'

'Forceful, maybe controlling,' she says. 'Does he ever tell you what to wear or how to be?'

Henry always picked my outfits. He'd told me what to wear since I'd let him into my head and I never once thought about how that might be weird. I'd never considered that it was forceful, I'd thought we were having fun together.

'Sometimes,' I hedge, unsure if I want to go down this route.

Dr Madison nods like she'd expected it. 'And did you ever stop to think that was quite controlling of Henry?'

'No,' I mumble. 'I'd never thought of it that way. It was just a bit of a laugh, that's all.'

'These things can start out that way,' she says. 'But there's often a darker side to them that's hidden and doesn't come out until much later. Telling you what to wear is a method of control, did you know that, Lydia?'

I shake my head. 'Henry doesn't control me,' I say, but the words don't taste right in my mouth. He'd controlled me a few times – slapped Pete, did my hair and make-up a certain way because I couldn't, ordered a drink I didn't want at the bar because he did. I try to shake off the uneasiness that's clawed its way into me, but it won't go away. Henry isn't a person, a distant part of me tells myself. Henry isn't like me or Pete or anyone else at school. He doesn't see things the way we do because he hasn't learnt how to yet.

'Did he ever make you do something you didn't want to do?'

I bring my knees to my chest as I think about what we did to Pete. Drugging him, cutting into his spine to put Henry's chip there so he could have a body. Dr Madison's questions make my insides twist.

The phone on her desk rings and makes us both jump.

She collects herself and answers the call. 'Hello? Right now? I'm in a session. Fine, give me a moment.' She stands up from the desk. 'Lydia, I have to see another patient for two minutes. Please excuse me.'

I nod as she leaves the room, and my eyes instantly go to her computer. I'm behind it before I've even registered crossing the room, completely uncaring that Agent Hall could be watching. It's been days since I touched a keyboard, heard a computer click in a way that tells me it's thinking. Code swims through my veins and pushes at my fingertips, begging to be let out.

My fingers type out an address. Pete's IP is returned to me in a millisecond. I link to his computer, force my way through his firewall and search his internet history to see if he's been online in the last few days. There are a few forums, porn sites, more hacker forums. I type out a new command. White lines of half-words and dashes pulse on the black background. It goes to Pete's webcam and brings up a live feed the way Henry would. I can see into Pete's room.

The curtains are drawn and the sheets on his bed are torn off the mattress, bundled into a messy heap. His swimming trophies and medals that once decorated his shelves now litter the floor. An empty wheelchair is at the foot of his bed. A *wheelchair*. I push myself away from the computer, nausea flooding my stomach. Did I do that to him? Did *we* do that to him?

I close everything down and shuffle back to the chesterfield. Dr Madison reappears a moment later. She apologizes for the interruption and comes to sit next to me.

'Now, where were we?'

'Actually, Dr Madison, I'd like to go back to my room now.'

Dr Madison's eyebrows rise. 'We still have twenty minutes, I thought we could—'

'Please.'

She runs her eyes over me, sees how I've twisted myself into a ball: my knees to my chin, my arms locked around my shins. I can't talk. Not right now. If I talk, I'll come undone, and Henry isn't here to put me back together.

Pete's in a wheelchair and it's all my fault. What's more, if he's at home and he can't walk, it means Henry's download never completed. Where is he now?

Dr Madison puts down her pad and escorts me from the room.

It was obvious bait, now that I think about it. Get me talking about Henry and leave me with an unattended computer. Does Agent Hall think I'm stupid enough to reach out to Henry somehow? I told him I would never give him up. I lie on my bed and gaze up at the tiled ceiling. Pete is in a wheelchair. How can I ever put that right?

Simon pokes his head around my door.

'Lydia, you have a phone call,' he says.

I sit up. 'Who is it?'

'They said it's a friend. Phone's at reception if you want to answer it,' he says, and leaves.

I follow after him, wondering who it could be. I didn't exactly have any friends other than Pete and now I know what happened to him, I'm not expecting him to call.

At reception, Simon busies himself unpacking a collection of needles and beakers and repacking them into another container. I pick up the plastic receiver, well aware my conversation is being monitored in more ways than one.

'Hello?' The receiver is warm against my ear, still hot from whoever used it last. No one says anything on the other end. All I can hear is a low buzz and heavy breathing. 'Hello?'

'Hi,' a voice says, and clears its throat.

'Who is this?'

'Emma. Parry. It's Emma.'

The last time I saw Emma she was spraying pink champagne at a screaming crowd. She probably saw me get arrested. Mum must have told her I'm here.

'Why are you calling me?'

'I wanted to see how you are,' she says after a moment.

'What do you really want, Emma?'

'All right,' she says. Her voice sounds strangled. 'It's my dad. He's gone. I wondered . . . if after everything . . . I know you're really good with computers. I was going to ask if you might be able to track him down.'

'I didn't think you got on with your dad. Why do you care where he is?'

'Some men came to the house – they were asking about money that's gone missing. Mum might get arrested because they can't find Dad. He put her name on a bunch of documents, but she says she never signed anything. I–I don't understand what's happening.'

We never looked at whose name was on the list of companies Mr Parry had created. If Henry knew Mrs Parry was going to take the rap, he never mentioned it to me. I pinch the bridge of my nose as the list of things Henry never cared about grows larger.

'I don't know for sure, but I can place a good bet on where your dad's gone,' I say.

'You can?' Emma says, her breath catching.

'I don't need a computer to tell me either,' I say, remembering how Henry and I had cancelled his plane ticket to the Caymans. He must have bought another ticket. 'How long's he been gone?'

'Four days. Those men came to the house looking for him not long after. Mum's locked herself in her bedroom and refuses to come out. Do you know where he is?'

'Yes.' I let a silence hang after my words. I chose not to publicize her nude selfies but that doesn't mean I have to help her out. If she hadn't bullied me, I might not be in a mental hospital right now.

'Please will you tell me?' she begs.

After everything Emma did, our plan to take Mr Parry's money had felt poetic. She'd messed with my family and I'd wanted to mess with hers. Henry had been curious if we could do it, and I'd wanted to know too.

Now I'm stuck in here, Henry is missing, and I'm not surprised to hear Mr Parry has gone to claim his hard-swindled cash.

I sigh. 'Do you know what your dad does for a living?'

'He's an accountant.'

'He's a con man,' I correct.

Emma is silent.

I eye Simon and turn away to whisper into the receiver. 'He sets up fake companies and tricks people out of their retirement funds. He's pocketed more than five million pounds, all transferred to a bank account in the Cayman Islands. I'll bet anything that's where he is.'

'I— Really? Are you sure?'

'Yep.' Henry had done a deep dive on Mr Parry's accounts.

'Does Mum know all this?'

'I don't know. The best thing you can do is report him to the police.'

'I think those men who came round *were* the police.'

'Call Interpol then, I'm sorry.'

Emma pauses. 'So am I. About everything. I know I said sorry in the club, but . . . I really mean it.'

I hesitate as I weigh her apology. She was the catalyst for my expulsion, but I would still have done well at my A-Levels, probably done well at whatever university I ended up at. I'd have carried on without my brother and without my dad because it's who I am. But Emma has scars she's still only just coming to terms with. It will be years before she's confident in her own skin, perhaps she never will, and I used her selfies to torment her.

'I'm sorry too,' I say. 'We got each other in pretty deep. Good luck with your dad.'

I hang up and run my fingers across my scalp. The guilt that has been plaguing me, following me around like a shadow, eases a little.

TWELVE

It doesn't matter how many press-ups or laps of the ward I do, I can't escape a date that looms over me like a distant storm. Soon it will be the sixth of April, and that means my brother will have been dead for two whole years.

Earlier in the week I worked out a length of the ward is a quarter of a mile. I run it four times, then eight, then twelve, and I collapse on my bed. Even before, if I were outside, I could never outrun this, but at least Henry might be able to distract me. Here, trapped in my cell-like room and without Henry at my side, the anniversary of my brother's death stares me in the face and begs me to address it.

On Friday, I have my usual morning session with Dr Madison. I eye the camera in the corner of her room. Its rounded black lens has been watching our sessions like a giant unblinking eye. Even though I suspect she's working for the people who imprisoned me, she's also the only one I can talk to. I tried talking to Maya, but she held up a hand and stopped me before we could get too personal. 'Can't get attached, can I?' she said. 'You'll be gone before I can ever leave and then where will I be? Will you come and visit on a Saturday like my parents?'

I swallowed and let her walk away. Everyone knows her parents never visit.

'I think I'm ready to talk about my brother,' I tell Dr Madison.

She leans forward. 'That's good, Lydia. That's real progress, well done. What do you want to talk about?'

'People don't understand,' I blurt. 'They think that after a funeral, after some grief counselling, we should forget about it and move on but it's not over and it'll never be over and how can you forget, anyway? How can you move on when your world is standing still?'

'Funerals do bring some measure of closure, but you are completely right,' Dr Madison says. 'It's not over simply because you've had a funeral.' She fetches a box of tissues and places it between us. I look at them with a mixture of hatred that I might need them and relief they're there in case I do.

'Mum bought these hideous flower arrangements that must have had about a hundred lilies in them and afterwards she left them all in our hallway. They stunk the house out for days and then all the orange stamens fell on the floor and Mum never got the stains out of the carpet. I hate lilies.'

Dr Madison nods as she listens. When I go quiet, she

prompts me, saying, 'Tell me about your brother. What was he like?'

'He loved animals,' I say at once. 'He wanted to be a vet. All his friends played computer games and went to football practice, but he was busy catching insects in the garden. Every year Mum and Dad would take us to the zoo for his birthday.'

Henry's birthday was in early-September when the weather was still decent. Trees still had fat leaves, dappled the gravel paths in green-sifted light. I can hear Henry's laugh as he raced me to the reptile house. He loved the alligators and lizards, who never seemed to do anything but lie there, but he didn't care. He lapped up the animals that did nothing. Everything was a treat to him, the world shiny and new like a banknote fresh off the press, not wrinkled and unspent in someone's moth-eaten pocket.

'He sounds lovely,' Dr Madison says.

'He was.'

I hate the past tense and how it means nothing good will ever happen again.

Dr Madison breaks the silence. 'Did you ever distract yourself from your brother's death? With your boyfriend, maybe?'

Building Henry had been mine and Dad's weekend project before my brother died, though I hadn't named him Henry at that point. A year and a half later, Dad left and Mum slumped into her mental absence, I'd continued to build Henry on my own. It had been a welcome distraction. Another year and a half passed in a blink. Henry took three years of late nights and early mornings, three years of patience and hard work and lines and lines of code and programming. As time went on, Henry had been the one I'd talked to, and he'd listened. He'd listened to everything.

People say I'm clever, but I didn't build Henry just because I was able to. I'd built him because I was lonely. He'd been my friend.

'Maybe,' I say.

'Perhaps it's time to deal with the loss,' Dr Madison says. 'How do you feel about your brother's death?'

'Sad. Guilty.'

'Why guilty?'

I look away. 'Isn't it normal to feel guilty when a family member dies?'

'It's very common, yes. I'm more interested in why *you* feel guilty.'

My fingers find a loose thread of skin at the base of a fingernail. I pull on it, watch the skin stretch white in protest. 'What if I'd sat behind Mum that day? And not behind Dad? It would have been me that died.'

'Ah, I see. We can drive ourselves to insanity with "what if" scenarios, you know.'

'But it's true. What if I'd been the one who died? Henry would be alive, not me. Mum and Dad might still be together.' I sink back into the chair, tugging on the piece of skin that refuses to part from its fleshy home. I twist it, coax it into a strand and pull.

'Is that important to you? Your parents being together?'

'Mum and Dad wanted Henry more than they wanted me,' I say. 'If Henry had survived then they would still be a family. I ruined it because I survived, not Henry.' I yank the strand of skin and wince at a flash of pain. I look down at the sphere of welling blood and try not to shudder.

'You don't know that,' Dr Madison says. 'You have no way of knowing what may have happened. You can torture yourself with as many of these scenarios as you can think of, but the fact remains you're here and Henry isn't. What happened with your parents was between them. It was nothing to do with you.'

Dad had looked at my eyes, my hair, all the features that told him I'm his and still walked away from me. He'd fallen in love with Mum because she was everything he wasn't. She used to always smile, could pull Dad out of his bad moods. He wanted Henry because he was like Mum. Dad didn't want me. He didn't want another version of himself.

I suck on the red pearl rising from my finger and swallow the metallic taste.

'Don't live in the past, Lydia. Therapists aren't supposed to give advice, but I will say that. You can't change the past. You can't change where you sat that day. Don't prolong your grief by punishing yourself for something you can't change.'

'How do you stop yourself from thinking about it over and over? Revisiting it in your dreams?'

Her smile pulls to one side. 'Time. And the more you talk about it, the more you'll be dealing with it. Your dreams are your brain's way of processing things. If you're not dealing with something on the outside, then the brain tries to deal with it on the inside. The more sessions we have like this where you open up, the easier it will get. In the meantime, it's okay to feel angry and frustrated.'

When the timer goes, Dr Madison leans off her elbow and smiles at me. 'You did very well today, Lydia.'

'When do you think I'll be able to leave?' I ask.

Dr Madison stands and goes back behind her desk. She takes her glasses off and I see the grooves the pads have left either side of her nose. Tiny pieces of plastic forever wearing down the skin the way secrets wear down a soul.

'We still have a lot to get through, Lydia,' she says. She tries a smile but I don't return it.

'Like what?'

'There's still a lot to be done.'

'Like *what*?'

'Lydia – one good therapy session is not enough to release you. I'm sorry, you will be here for a while longer.'

'How long?'

'Probably a year, at least.'

'A year? You just said I'd made progress.'

Dr Madison gives a short sigh. 'As sad as losing your brother was, you're not in here because of it. You're in here because you let your anger rule your actions. You imprisoned your mother and gravely injured a boy from your school. That is why you are here.'

I open and close my mouth. Pete's in a wheelchair because of me. The guilt I've been carrying around, the same way someone else might carry a backpack, doubles. It slips its wraith-like fingers into the gaps between my bones and pulls until I ache all over.

I look down at my hands. 'I'm dealing with my anger as best as I can.'

'I know,' she says. 'I hear a lot about your press-ups and running, it sounds like you're doing well. If you keep it up, you might be out in less than a year.'

Less than a year still sounds like most of a year to me, and Dr Madison looks at me like she knows my thoughts. I agreed to come here to protect Henry, but the truth is I've done some horrible things and I deserve to be here. For the first time since I began therapy, I start crying.

Dr Madison is at my side in a second and thrusts a tissue into my hands. I take it and curl myself into a ball, pressing my eyes into my knees as silent shudders surge through my body.

'I'm sorry,' I say, my apology a muffled wet snort. 'I'm so sorry for all of it.'

Dr Madison looks at me with kind eyes. 'It's okay, Lydia. Let it out.'

When the session comes to a close and Simon appears at the door, she waves him away and walks me back to the ward herself.

'Don't be ashamed of your tears,' she tells me on the way. 'Feeling means growth, remember.'

'Growth sucks.'

She chuckles as we come to a stop outside the ward doors. 'It's often painful, yes. But it's important you know your tears are never wasted. If you feel guilty about what happened, it means you're accepting responsibility for it.' She looks me in the eye. 'But don't accept responsibility for things that are not your fault,' she says. 'Like where you sat that day – that's not your fault.'

I nod, wiping my nose on the back of my hand because my tissue is too damp to be useful. My desire to get revenge on Emma was tangled in Henry's desire to upgrade himself further, and the two became so blurred that I lost track of where I did things for Henry and where I did things for myself. Henry didn't know the rightness or wrongness of what we were doing, but I don't have that excuse. I knew and did it anyway.

If he were here, Henry would know what to say to make me feel better. He'd show me a memory I've forgotten or twine his invisible fingers through my hair and stroke away the sadness. Instead, Dr Madison squeezes my shoulder and releases me into the ward. It's the nicest physical contact I've had with anyone since I got here. It makes me long for more.

In my room, I stand on my tiptoes on the bed to look out of my barred window. Beyond the chain-link fence, spring is flaring into being. Branches are fuller, showing off leaves and shoots of colour. I finger the scab on the back of my arm as I look at it all and wonder when I'll be able to go out there and walk among it.

*

Henry walks towards me, tall, clean-shaven. I can make out his square jaw, his white smile and Roman nose, but he's blurry at the same time. Hazy, shrouded in fog, because he's conjured from my shifting imagination. He closes the distance between us and brings his mouth to mine. I fall into his kiss.

He pulls away and goes over to a new Mercedes. I stand with my hand outstretched, willing him to come back to me with my eyes because my voice won't work.

'Soon,' he says, and drives away.

THIRTEEN

On Saturday, Maya slinks into my room with a smile. She cosies up next to me while I'm sat on my bed and wraps her arms around me in a hug. As she does, she slides a cloth bag under my pillow. I palm her a sock filled with tablets I'd faked swallowing. 'You get caught using that, you did not get it from me. You get me?' She kisses me on the cheek and then leaves.

I take my bartered item out from its hiding place. It's a penknife, smooth and plastic until I flick up the ragged blade, good enough to cut through an inch-thick fillet steak. The tip pricks my fingertip easily. I clamp a tissue around the nick and try not to think about it.

My plan for escape makes me laugh. Cut the wires in the access-control box and set off the door's auto-release, but then what? I'd probably trigger a handful of alarms. I've seen the other orderlies from time to time, and they're all built like Simon: wide and impassable. Getting through the door is one thing, getting past *them* is something else.

I think about my brother. What happened to him was awful, but it wasn't my fault. Dr Madison made me realize I'd been carrying the responsibility for his death around with me the way someone might haul around a suitcase. It's horrible that he died and I didn't, but it wasn't anyone's fault.

What I did to Pete was my fault.

I hide the penknife against the length of my forearm, securing it in place with a couple of hairbands and a tight sleeve. It's too risky to leave lying around – the nurses like to do 'random checks' that are absolutely not random at all. The plastic is cool against my skin and I fidget to get used to it.

Simon makes me jump as he pokes his head around my door. 'You have a visitor, Lydia.'

The news makes me frown. 'Who?'

'I'll meet you by the door in five minutes.'

I go straight to the doors – there's nothing else to do – and wait for him. The red light on the box to the side of the doors continues to blink away, governing my life unknowingly. The tip of my knife could sever the plastic parts. The sharp teeth could bite into the plastic cables, cut them to shreds and override the auto-lock so the doors clank open. I could do it now. Let everyone escape. Let pandemonium ensue as the town learns several mental patients are on the loose.

Then what? I'd probably be caught. End up locked in here for even longer. I have to pick the right moment, if it ever comes.

'Ready?' Simon comes to my side, breaking me from my daydream.

I nod and let him take me down the corridor to the visitors' rooms.

I'm not sure who to expect. I have no friends who would want to visit and Mum hasn't called since I was incarcerated. When I step into the room, my breath hitches.

'Well now. Good morning, Phelps,' Agent Hall says.

Sitting down opposite him, I take a deep breath. It's been seven days since I had contact with Henry, and it was Agent Hall who oversaw my incarceration. He trapped me in here for refusing to let him dissect Henry like a laboratory frog.

'How are you finding everything?'

'Fabulous,' I say. 'Why are you here?'

'I wanted to drop by,' he drawls, his blue eyes burning into mine. Summer-sky blue. I shiver. 'See how you were doing. Wondered if you'd like to reconsider my offer.' He places a familiar-looking manila file on the desk between us. It's thicker than the last time I saw it, and I wonder what else Agent Hall has discovered I've done. Henry falsified too many travel documents to count. Passports, plane tickets, driving licences . . .

'I thought it was one-time only?'

Agent Hall shifts. 'This is a new offer. In this one, you would be allowed out of Grenville Psych to come to work with SSP where we would keep a very close eye on you. There you would assist us in decoding your Artificial

Intelligence and helping us build our own. As soon as the project ends, you'd be brought back here.'

A flare of excitement races through me. They have Henry's chip. That means Agent Hall must have already tried to break into it. I study the bags under his eyes and his unshaven jaw. SSP can't have got very far for Agent Hall to be sat in front of me.

'You must really need me.'

Agent Hall sneers. 'If you don't fancy a change of scenery, I can leave you to it.'

I lean back in my chair. 'But then you'll never know why the chip won't work.'

'Why won't it work?'

I shrug and look at my fingernails. I've picked the skin around them to red scabs since I've been admitted to Grenville Psych. 'You're going to have to improve your offer, Hall.'

He flips an anti-static bag on to the table. There's something small inside. Henry. My heartbeat spikes and I reach to grab it but Agent Hall's hand slams down on it first.

'I thought you weren't interested?'

'I'm listening,' I say, not taking my hand away.

'Why doesn't it work, Phelps? Doesn't matter how many things we hook it up to, we can't get in.'

I remember the special wire Henry ordered to connect the chips together. Maybe it got lost somewhere between Pete's transportation from Glimmer to the hospital. Something tells me Henry's secret design was not an accident.

'Let me see what damage you've done.'

Agent Hall relents and his hand releases the chip.

Blood rushes through my ears and my heart beats so loud I'm sure Agent Hall can hear it.

I pick up the anti-static bag, force the tremble from my fingers. The chip looks intact on the exterior. Any traces of Pete's body have been cleaned away. All twelve legs look straight. If Henry didn't transfer to Pete, he must still be in his chip. There's only one way to know for sure.

Agent Hall busies himself by removing his jacket and rolling up his sleeves. I may not have another chance.

I jump up and ram my chair under the door handle. Agent Hall looks up as I remove the knife from its hiding place along the inside of my arm. The blade glints as it flicks upright. He leaps across the room as it cuts into my forearm. I hold back a retch as blood pours instantly from the cut. So red. Agent Hall grapples with my knife hand. Blood trickles down my arm and blooms on the white cotton of his shirt sleeve.

'Give me the knife, Phelps.'

'No.' I fumble to get the chip out of its bag with my other hand.

Agent Hall yells for help and an orderly is at the window behind me in a second. The door handle won't budge under the chair holding it in place. He bangs on the window and Hall tries to wrestle the knife from my clutches. My grip is strong, fingers wrapped around the handle. It's been seven days without Henry, I won't let him go so easily.

I stamp on Hall's foot; he gasps loudly and his grip on my wrist slackens. I try to twist the knife away from him, but it catches the skin of his forearm in the struggle. The blade rakes across his arm, and I feel the sickening vibration of the serrated blade as it opens his flesh. He cries out and backs away.

Code through the problem, Lydia. Not around it.

I look from my arm to his arm, study our matching wounds. He locked me up in here to force me into giving him Henry. I still don't know what SSP intends to do with Henry, with me. There's only one way to find out.

Agent Hall can only be about two years older than me, but he's broad and muscular. There's no way I can take him down, no matter how many press-ups I've been doing. Surprise is all I have. I run at him, shove him against the far wall. His hands come to my face to push me off, but I bite his fingers. He loses his balance and falls to the floor. His head hits the ground with a dull smack. He groans.

The orderly bangs against the door, the handle jerking. In the distance, an alarm blares. I block it all out. I'm so close to having Henry back.

More blood drips from Agent Hall's arm and spatters on to the floor. My stomach knots and I clench my teeth together. I will not let my fears stand in my way.

Agent Hall fights as I clamber on top of him to put all my weight against his bleeding arm. His breath is hot against my ear and he cries out when I force the chip into his cut. I ram it all the way in, watch the flesh part to make room for Henry's chip. I've done most of the work; it won't need to burrow so far. I keep my weight on Agent Hall's arm and he yells again. It's a yell I remember all too well from when my own chip reacted to my body. How it found a sweet spot to nestle into and hide in, selecting the best place for Henry to hack into my nervous system.

Hall screams and I savour the noise. He locked me away so he could force me into giving him Henry. Now he'll get to know Henry on a more intimate level.

Agent Hall knees me in the side and I roll over with a gasp. He backs away, clawing at his arm. Streaks of blood cover the white floors and his chest. I can see every taut tendon in his neck, every rigid muscle in his arm as he fights the chip that tunnels into it.

The chair collapses behind me and two orderlies rush in. They seize me, pin my arms behind my back and slam me to the floor as they yank down my joggers and jam a needle in my bum. The room darkens as they drag me from it. The last thing I see is Agent Hall passed out against the far wall.

If Henry's still in there, I've done all I can.

PART THREE

FOURTEEN

Solitary confinement consists of a room not big enough to do a star jump in. There's a bed attached to the wall and a toilet at the end of it. That's it. That's all you get when you're being punished. I've been told I'll be staying here indefinitely, and that any further visits will be supervised by Simon or another orderly. It doesn't matter. There won't be any other visits.

One of the nurses had come to the window in the door to pass me my dinner tray last night.

'How's Agent Hall?' I'd asked, curious to hear if he'd woken up feeling any different.

She'd pursed her lips and closed the window without replying.

I bash my head against the wall. No windows to the outside world. No contact. No news of Henry.

When I'd put Henry's chip in my arm, it had taken him twenty minutes to hack into me, to link with my neural pathways. Something must have gone wrong.

Maybe the reason SSP couldn't tap into Henry's chip in the first place was because his program never transferred to it correctly. Henry could be lost. Gone for ever.

A new, far worse thought occurs to me. If Henry's chip works and he's taken control of Agent Hall, he won't need me any more. He'll have his own body. He can do his own thing, plan his own hacks, have his own life. Maybe he only pretended to care about me while I was useful to him. And now I'll rot in Grenville Psych for the rest of my life and he won't even come to visit on a Saturday.

No. Henry said he'd never leave me. I don't know if that's the same thing as love to Henry, but I do know he's never broken his word. Whatever Henry put his mind to, he accomplished.

I trust his word. He *will* come for me.

Simon appears at the door to give me my sleeping tablets. When I hold out my hand, he takes my arm through the window. I yelp as he sticks a needle into the skin, and his firm grip on my bandaged forearm makes my knife-cut ache.

'What? No tablets?'

'Not for the moment,' he says. 'You're to have yours via injection until you can be trusted again.'

By 'trusted' I understand Simon means 'not to give them to anyone else in exchange for sharp objects'. I hope Maya isn't too furious.

Drowsiness seeps through my veins and I lie back on the bed with a yawn. There's no window to confirm it, but it feels like night-time.

The lights flicker on and off. I blink awake, and they do it again. The heavy door opposite me clanks as it releases and swings open. I sit up as a broad-shouldered silhouette appears in my doorway. Squinting, I can see he has hair as dark as the corridor behind him, and his blue-eyed gaze burns as he looks me over.

'Lydia.'

It's Agent Hall. He comes to my bedside and kneels to my level. I trace his face with my eyes, sweeping over the heated blue irises to the square line of his jaw. He reaches for my hand and his touch sends a whisper up my arm, nudging the chip that hasn't buzzed for days.

'Henry?'

He smiles, and his fingers come to my cheek to brush away a fallen tear.

'Hi,' he says. His voice is deep. I want to fall into it, never forget it.

'Is this a dream?' I feel stupid for asking but I've wanted Henry for so long. My dreams with him felt so real, I'm not sure if he's really here.

'No,' he says, cupping my face. 'I am here.'

His palm is smooth and fits the curve of my cheek. I nod, swallow down a cry. He's here. 'I knew you'd come for me.' The lump in my throat makes my words come out in a choke.

'I said I would never leave you. I am only sorry it took me so long to get back to you.'

My body trembles and I clamp my mouth shut to stop

a sob escaping. 'I thought I'd lost you,' I say when I find my voice again. 'I thought your program was gone for good.'

'I am here, Lyd,' Henry says. 'What do you think?' He smiles, blue eyes round and vulnerable for a moment.

Agent Hall was older than me and he's over six feet tall. Somewhere in the back of my mind I register that Henry isn't speaking how Agent Hall used to. He sounds the way he did in my head. It suits him.

I lean forwards and press my lips to his. He tastes salty, and I realize I'm still crying. Henry breathes deeply, inhaling me. His arms come around my back. When he releases me, we both gasp. His touch is how it was when he was inside my head, fingers trilling over my skin, waking every nerve and setting them on fire.

'You do not know how long I have wanted to do that.'

I smile. 'Yes, I do.'

Henry stands me up and leads me from the room. The corridor lights sputter into life as we walk along it, extinguishing behind us one by one as we go. It's strange holding Henry's hand – his touch finally given a physical presence. I squeeze it as he leads me down the corridor and he squeezes back. A pulse travels up my arm and nudges the chip there. My bare feet pad along the tiles and I shrink behind Henry as we near the security station. Henry pulls me past it, not stopping to slow down.

'I looped the feed. No one can see us.'

Around the corner, the security guard is slumped over his desk. A mug is on the floor, spilt coffee a sticky brown

212

pool at his feet. The guard groans and tries to stand. Henry drops my hand in an instant and makes his way over to the guard. He forces the guard on to his knees, one hand inching closer to the man's neck.

'Don't kill him!'

Henry looks up at me. His hand pauses close to the thick neck he probably knows a thousand ways to snap.

'It would be easier,' he says. 'Then he would not be able to report you as missing.'

The way Henry's head tilts a little to the left, and the way his eyebrows tighten the smallest degree tells me he thinks he's right. Dr Madison was right. Without guilt, Henry can do whatever he wants. There's still so much he doesn't understand.

'No,' I tell him. 'No killing. We don't kill.'

Henry takes a moment to consider what I'm saying, and then whacks the guard on the back of the head. He crumples to the floor. I rush over and slip two fingers under his flabby jawline. Relief seeps through me as my fingertips locate the soft beat of his pulse.

'I did not kill him,' Henry says.

'I just wanted to check.'

He pulls me along the corridor towards the double-doored exit. I stop and stare at it. The flashing red light turns green under Henry's silent instruction. My entire existence here was dictated by these doors, and he only needs to blink at them to bend them to his will. I clutch Henry's hand harder. He's really here. He's getting me out.

As we slip down flights of stairs, Henry's eyes flicker. Doors unlock as we approach them. If I had tried to escape on my own, each one would have been a stumbling block. But Henry only needs to look at them.

Outside, headlights accelerate down the drive towards us. There's a smash as a vehicle careens through the security barrier, and a guard leans out of the booth and yells. The car heads straight for us. I step back, but Henry doesn't move an inch. The car swerves and halts in a muted screech. It's a BMW, one of the smaller electric models.

Henry answers my raised eyebrow with a smile and says, 'It was in a car park near Agent Hall's hotel in Grenville. I used it to get here.' He opens my door and closes it behind me before running around and seating himself behind the wheel.

'Do you know how to drive?' I ask.

'I know how to hack it.'

'That's not what I asked.'

'Put your seat belt on,' Henry instructs, one hand on the wheel as the silent engine takes us back down the driveway. I'm not sure where he learnt, but at least he understands we drive on the left.

Henry clicks his belt into place. The steering wheel rotates as if his hands were still on it. He reaches over and kisses my cheek. 'I have missed you.'

'Do you know it's been over a week?'

'It did not feel like that long to me.' His free hand crosses the gap between our seats and rests on my thigh. 'I am sorry for what happened to you while I was offline. Agent Hall filled me in on much of what I missed.'

'He wanted to find out how you're made, Henry.'

'I know, I can read his mind.'

'We need to go far away,' I say, 'so no one can find us.' But that isn't the only reason. If we go far away, I can teach him right from wrong, guilt and empathy, and how to be a better person.

'I will book new plane tickets for the Cayman Islands. We can go from London, it is more direct.'

'Can you find us somewhere safe to hide before the flight? Somewhere low-key?'

Henry's eyes glitter. 'I am booking a hotel.'

'There's someone I need to see before we go.' I stare off at the passing streetlights. 'I think he's in a wheelchair now. He might not be able to walk again.'

'I am unsure what you hope to achieve by seeing him,' Henry says.

'I just have to see, all right?'

At a roundabout, Henry indicates right and goes all the way round, back towards Grenville.

FIFTEEN

I fidget the entire way to Pete's house. It's somewhere I've been dozens of times, down an estate I know well, but I can't help looking over my shoulder as I go to his front door. Another SSP agent could be hiding in the dark. It was a risk to come here, but I have to know if the damage I caused is permanent. The door's locked, but Henry throws a glance at the alarm and picks the lock without any wailing repercussions. I wonder if Agent Hall knew how to pick locks and that's how Henry knows.

Henry waits in the hallway while I creep up the stairs to Pete's bedroom and peer around the door. Last time I saw his room all his swimming trophies were toppled over on the floor. Now they're not there at all. A wheelchair is a dark silhouette at the end of his bed.

Pete is awake. He's sat up in bed, keyboard on his lap, and his skin looks pale in the blue light from the nearby monitor swivelled his way. He tries to sit up straighter when I walk in. I go straight over and clamp my hand over his mouth. He struggles against me but it's not as hard as it used to be to push him off.

'I'm not here to hurt you,' I tell him.

His breath is short and hot against my hand but eventually it calms, and I release him. I sit on the edge of his bed, where he had once forced me to sit.

'Why aren't you locked away?' he says.

'I came to apologize.'

Pete laughs. It's the kind of laugh that has no humour. He glares at me. 'Get. Out.'

I stand up, look down at him. There are dark shadows under his eyes. His legs are at an awkward angle underneath his quilt. It's an effort to swallow and say, 'I wanted to say I'm sorry, about your legs. Is it . . . is it permanent?'

'They don't know.'

All I can do is nod. The chip would have been buried so deep in his spinal cord I'm surprised they managed to remove it at all. His days as an amateur swimmer are over.

Pete shakes his head. 'You're not sorry at all. You came to see what you did.'

'No, I would never—'

'I knew you were fucked up, Lydia. As soon as I started at school everyone told me how weird you were because of your dead brother, but I thought we could be friends.'

Anger flares inside of me. 'Friends don't lie about stuff to get into the popular crowd. Friends don't get each other drunk and try to come on to them,' I snap back.

'I wouldn't have done anything you didn't want to do,'

he mumbles. His nostrils flare as his anger quickly replaces his embarrassment. 'But what about when you came over and kissed me on the doorstep? You wanted to then. And don't forget it was *you* who tricked *me* at Glimmer.'

I run my hands through my hair. This isn't how this was supposed to go. 'Look, I'm sorry. Really sorry. Everything got out of hand for me and I'm trying to put it right.'

'You can never put it right!' Pete shouts, face red. I cringe at the possibility his mum might barge in at any moment.

Henry appears at the door and Pete turns to him in surprise. 'What are you doing here?' he asks.

I pause, looking over at Henry who stares back with blue eyes that make my heartbeat falter. Pete still thinks it's Agent Hall, but there's no time to explain.

'Lydia, we should leave,' he says.

I nod and wipe my eyes. Henry was right. I never should have come. Some dark part of me had needed to see the repercussions of what I'd done, the irreparable chaos I'd caused because I let Henry go too far.

'I'm sorry,' I whisper to Pete.

'Get out,' he snarls.

I follow Henry from the bedroom, down the stairs and out of the house. Rain spatters his face and splits his hair into dark chunks. There's an overwhelming ache inside me that won't go away. I ruined Pete's life. He might never walk again.

Henry pulls me close to him. He strokes my soaked hair as I press my eyes so hard to his chest they might push back into my skull. After a moment, he takes me back to the car and straps me in. We drive in silence for a moment, and I think of Pete as Henry hacks into something unknown. I yawn and rub my puffy eyes. The meds are still in my system, and crying has made my head ache.

'You should sleep, Lyd,' Henry says.

'I'm scared,' I whisper.

'What of?'

'More nightmares,' I say.

Henry leans over to kiss my nose. I want to pull him down into me and hold him there for ever. 'I will be here if you have one.'

I curl up in my seat and doze in and out of consciousness. Henry drives with one hand on the wheel and the other holds my hand in my lap. His eyes are far away, and I wonder if he's only gripping the wheel in case anyone sees him driving with no hands. The engine is a silent cocoon and nudges me back into sleep.

SIXTEEN

wake again when we arrive at a service station. Dawn is a shell-pink over encroaching black hills.

'Where are we?' I murmur.

'East of Birmingham,' Henry says, as he leans over to unfasten my seat belt. 'We still have some way to go but I thought you would like some breakfast.'

We head into the service station main building to find a toilet. There aren't many people around, but those that are stare at my bare feet. At least Henry looks relatively normal in a shirt and trousers, even if his rolled-up sleeve is covered in blood and his arm is bandaged up to the elbow. Looking around, there are no shops selling shoes or clothing of any kind. I ignore the glances from total strangers and continue through the food court to the toilets.

I splash water on my face and under my arms when no one's looking. I promise myself the first thing I'll do when we get to the hotel is have a real shower.

Henry waits for me outside the toilet. A dark shadow clings to his jaw and I wonder what it would feel like to run my hands over it. He looks good. A squirm works into my stomach at the thought of how much he feels like Henry. I squash down a pang of guilt about Agent Hall. Where is he now?

'What do you want for breakfast?' Henry asks, taking my hand as we go to the food court. There are several people sat with their meals, inhaling their teas and coffees. I'm settling on a McDonald's breakfast when an oversized TV catches my eye. Henry is still as he watches it too.

My face stares back at me from the screen.

'. . . Phelps, a young escapee from a psychiatric unit in Grenville, Cheshire. The BBC would like to remind the public that Miss Phelps has recently attacked an individual and is to be considered dangerous. Police advise calling their helpline rather than attempting to apprehend her yourself. Phelps is thought to be travelling with an accomplice, Mr Andrew Hall, who is also known to the police . . .'

Henry's face flashes on the screen next to mine. A phone number scrolls beneath it in a large red font.

'That number diverts to SSP headquarters,' Henry tells me, his eyes flickering as he traces it on his contacts.

My stomach flips and I shrink against Henry's solid torso. When we'd arrived, people were staring at me, but I thought it was because I wasn't wearing shoes. Someone could have recognized us. We could have been on the TV the entire time we were driving and not known about it. I look at our pictures. Mine's an old school picture from when my hair was cropped to my jaw and my skin was misbehaving. Henry looks younger, mid-teens. His hair's longer and he's clean-shaven. Out of both of us, he's the least recognizable. I wonder if his not shaving is purposeful.

On screen, the news anchor is arguing with someone talking over her in the background. The picture changes to Dr Madison getting out of her car at Grenville Psych. She slams her car door shut.

'For the last time, I cannot discuss individual cases, there is a clear law of doctor and patient con—'

The reporter ignores the predictable response. 'Regardless of confidentiality, one of your patients is on the loose. Just how secure is your facility? The public deserve an explanation.'

'I appreciate your concern, but our patients have families that deserve their privacy too. Please leave the facility's grounds. Good morning.'

The news anchor shuffles her papers and turns to a different camera. 'That was Dr Madison at Grenville Psychiatric Unit in Cheshire. Join us later when we discuss the escapee with her headmaster, Mr Cramer. We turn now to our mental health correspondent, Dr Singh. Doctor, what can you tell us about Lydia Phelps and her mental state?'

I turn to Henry. 'Henry, we're all over the news. Even you.'

'I am dealing with it.' He pulls me close and I watch as the TV stutters with static. Our pictures disappear from the side of the screen and then all the on-screen graphics fail. The news anchor presses a finger to her ear.

'Excuse me, Doctor, one moment. We appear to be having some technical difficulties. I'll read that number aloud for anyone who may have information. That's ...'

Henry blinks and the TV changes channel. It's the ITV news showing an image of me – the same school picture as before – and Henry's face flashes up next to it. Henry frowns and his eyes flicker as he hacks his way into the news channel. The TVs around the room jitter for a few seconds before being overtaken by the grey and white stutter of static.

Henry rubs the back of my neck. 'It is done. I have removed us from other news channels as well.'

His words aren't as comforting as he means them to be. Being on the BBC and ITV was bad enough, let alone *other* news channels. Looking around, I can see several cameras perched up high and pointed at the food court seating area. Anyone could be watching.

'What about the CCTV in here?'

'I cut it when we pulled up.' He looks down at me and smiles. 'It will be okay, Lyd. I will deal with SSP. What do you want for breakfast?'

My insides are flat and empty, but I can't stomach the thought of food. Henry tells me I must eat something, and orders us both porridge to go and a black coffee for himself. While we wait, I feel like all the people around us are staring. I shrink into Henry's side, turn away from anyone who comes near. Henry squeezes my shoulder and all the TVs in the food court turn off completely. People nearby look up from their breakfasts with confusion.

'Do not worry.'

On the way out, Henry steers me towards a new car. It's a Tesla parked in one of the charging spots, and it unlocks as we walk towards it.

'Whose car is that?' I ask.

'Mine,' Henry says. 'I bought it and had it delivered here.' He runs his hand over the car door before opening it for me. His eyes glitter as he hacks into something else, and I wonder what he's up to.

'Where did you get the money for this, Henry?'

'Anywhere I want.' He notices my frown. 'Do not worry. It is untraceable.'

'We're keeping a low profile, right?' I ask, when we're both inside and he's in the driver's seat.

'Yes. None of my purchases are large enough to raise any interest.'

I swallow a mouthful of scalding-hot porridge. If he doesn't consider a car to be a large purchase, what else has he bought? 'What purchases?' I choke.

'You will see.'

He takes a sip of his black coffee and I wonder how he knew he would like it. Once, on an episode of *24 Hours in A&E*, the recipient of a kidney transplant developed an appetite for foods he'd never liked before. Mum told me they could have been things the donor liked. Was Agent Hall a fan of black coffee?

Henry catches me watching him. 'What?'

'I hate coffee.'

Henry smiles into his cup. 'I like it. Tea is horrible.'

'You never said anything when I drank it before!'

'I did not want to tell you what to drink,' Henry says, laughing.

'You ordered that Martini for me in Glimmer without asking,' I say, remembering Dr Madison's warning that Henry is controlling. 'And told me what to wear, ordered me a dress and shoes and everything. Why did you do that?'

Henry frowns and he abandons the wheel completely to give me his full attention. I try not to look at how we manoeuvre between the parked cars as we go on to a main road.

'Was that wrong of me?'

'Yes . . . No. I don't know. Why did you do it?'

'You are beautiful, Lydia. I feel . . . very strongly for you.' His cheeks turn pink as he speaks. I didn't know an AI could blush, but he has his own body now. 'I wanted to see what you looked like in some things. I am sorry.'

Dr Madison had warned me Henry's behaviour was controlling, but I can see from how embarrassed Henry is he never meant it like that. He never picked my outfits to control me. He did it because he didn't know how else to express his feelings.

'Maybe next time you could ask?' I say. 'I like picking my outfits too.'

'Of course.' He leans over to kiss my cheek. 'I am sorry. I will not do it again.'

I nod and we're silent for a moment as Henry turns back to the wheel.

After a while, he says, 'We need to disappear, Lyd. How do you feel about going blonde?'

I pull down the visor and look at my reflection in the mirror. 'I don't want to look like my mother.'

He laughs. 'You will never look like her.'

'What about red?' I twist a lock of hair around my finger. 'I could pull that off.'

'You could pull anything off.' Little lights dance across his eyes as he pulls up a website to make me an appointment.

I relax into chatting with Henry again. It's strange hearing his voice out loud, the voice I knew so well in my head finally given a physical representation. It's deep and rumbly, not like Agent Hall whose words were laced with tricks and smarm. Henry talks the same way as he did on his old unit and in my head. I remember when I'd first started talking to him, asking him questions to check he was responding properly. He didn't understand compound words. When I'd upgraded him and he'd learnt how to use them, he didn't want to. It wasn't his voice.

'How come it took so long for you to come and get me?' I ask. 'It only took you twenty minutes to hack into me.'

'I am sorry for making you wait. I did not take control of Agent Hall straight away,' Henry says. 'I wanted to see what he was doing, what he was planning. I can read his mind the way I could read yours when we were linked. Hall was going to go to the hospital and get the chip taken out, so I was forced to assume control. I put a pair of contacts in and then came to find you.'

'Did he tell SSP what happened?'

'Yes. They were very interested to hear he was not damaged. They thought he would be hurt like Pete. Hall thought my chip was broken or not programmed correctly.'

I share a smirk with Henry.

'Thank you for rescuing me,' I say.

'I am sorry you ended up in there for me.'

'You would have done it for me.'

'I would,' Henry says, and he lets the car do the driving for a moment as he drinks his coffee.

I reach out and stroke the back of his head, weave my fingers between the short dark hairs. A daunting thought penetrates my mind and wells there. Henry is unique. He has likes and dislikes now more than ever. My plan had been to find him, and if I couldn't, recreate him somehow. But each program that made Henry – the very order of each keystroke in all his lines of code – would have been impossible to recreate exactly. There's only one Henry and I'd come so close to losing him.

He's here because he promised he'd never leave me. He came for me, as he said he would. Though I'm still unsure just what he is, I know one thing for certain: Henry wants me.

I want him too.

SEVENTEEN

Nothing stays still for long in the centre of London. People walk out in front of us if they think they can make it to the other side of the road, and Henry obeys every traffic light, trapping us for minutes at junctions. He says he could change them but he doesn't want to bring attention to us. There are cameras above every light, on every street corner. Cyclists are everywhere and pedestrians all seem to either smoke or be in a hurry. After living alone with Mum in our big house for so long, London feels claustrophobic. We're bumper to bumper the whole way to the hotel.

When Henry pulls up outside the Rosehall Hotel, I pinch myself to check I'm not still at Grenville Psych experiencing a sleeping-drug-fuelled dream. A wrought-iron gate swings open for us off the High Holborn Road, and we drive in. It's like driving into a secret in the middle of a city. Every metre of the open courtyard is a jewel amidst buildings built in each other's shadows.

Pristine off-white stone swoops into curves and inlaid columns, and trimmed topiary boxes adorn every sash window.

'I said somewhere low-key,' I hiss.

Henry shrugs as he puts Agent Hall's jacket on, hiding his bloody sleeves. 'There is hardly any CCTV.'

'I'm sure there are plenty of B & Bs with no CCTV,' I say, when he collects me from my side of the car. He holds my hand as we walk to the front door.

'Yes. I like this option better.'

The doorman eyes Henry and then me for a few seconds that feel like years. Why is it whenever we turn up somewhere, I look like a bedraggled rat and Henry looks normal? I'm still wearing a tattered long-sleeved top and jogger bottoms that ripped when I got a needle in the bum. I don't have any shoes on. I look like what I am: an escaped mental patient. I try to relax in the knowledge that Henry wouldn't take me anywhere we'd be recognized. The fact the doorman won't let us in is for completely different reasons. Henry raises an eyebrow and coughs. The doorman fixes a smile and opens the door for us.

The black and white entrance hall smells of floor wax and the glittering chandelier is as big as my house. Bouquets of Stargazer lilies decorate the tables, their heavy stench clogging the nearby air. I shrink as I see them, and Henry squeezes my hand.

'I know, Lyd,' he says. He can read my mind even when we're not connected.

He pulls me towards the reception desk. 'I have a reservation under Smith. I requested an early check-in,' he tells the receptionist. The man looks at me and back at Henry. 'And I will be paying in cash.' Henry deposits a thick roll of twenties on the desk. I stare at the money. It's more than I've seen in one place before. I die a little inside as the receptionist gives me a proper once-over. I look like Henry has found me on the street, he's clearly given a fake name and he's paying for everything in cash. Heat creeps up my neck and into my face.

'Certainly, sir,' the receptionist says smoothly. 'I will still require an ID.'

Henry hands over a driver's licence and the receptionist disappears to a back room. When he reappears, he passes Henry a key card and directs us to a lift. As Henry starts explaining about a delivery, I glance around the entrance hall. Near to the door, a man and a woman smirk with each other and share a kiss. He whispers in her ear, and she pushes him lightly on the arm as though he's said something outrageous. I watch them both giggle at a joke I can't hear. The way her long hair falls to her waist and how he flashes her an easy grin makes me wonder at how trouble-free their relationship must be. They step into the sunshine of the courtyard and disappear behind the closing door.

I look back at Henry thumbing his way through someone else's wallet, someone else's blood soaked into his sleeve. Will our relationship ever be as free or without shadows?

'Ready?' Henry asks.

I nod, and he guides me across the black and white tiles, his hand on the small of my back like I'm wearing a sweeping ball gown, not tattered sweats. I sink into the gesture, my heartbeat calming at his touch. We might never be like that other couple, but Henry always knows how to make me feel wanted.

We watch the skyline of London descend as we rise in the lift. Roads and side roads bleed across the city, and the Thames glitters in a ponderous curve through it all.

Henry holds me to his side and kisses my temple. He leads the way to the room, my fingers laced in his as I trail after him. He doesn't look at the door numbers; I know he's pulled up a schematic, using that to find his way around instead. I miss having Henry inside my head, projecting on to my contact lenses and hooking me up to everything.

He doesn't bother to use the key card. The door of our room opens as he blinks at it and he steps back to let me walk in first.

A hallway with a deep carpet greets my Grenville Psych-hardened feet. It opens up into a living room with over-padded cushions on all the striped sofas and armchairs. A dark wooden bar owns the left-hand corner, and soft lighting from standing lamps fills the room. Everything points towards a seventy-inch 8K TV. Beyond, a sizeable balcony overlooks a skyline that sparkles, dominated by the Gherkin building.

In the room to the left, a huge bed fills the room,

covered in crisp white sheets and more pillows than I can count. I freeze when I look at it. There's only one bed.

I jump when Henry comes up behind me. I don't look but I know he's eyeing the bed too. He kisses the side of my head and tells me my salon appointment is in twenty minutes. He heads to the bar in the living room, and I wash my face and look longingly at the shower but there's not enough time. Henry tells me he ordered clothes from ASOS for us on a six-hour delivery when we were driving down. He tells me I can pick whatever I want, and we'll send the rest back. I understand even he can't magic clothes out of thin air, but I'm sad to go to the salon wearing my ripped joggers and no shoes.

I go into the living room where Henry sits at the bar sipping a Vesper Martini. I wrap my arms around myself.

'What is wrong?'

I tug at my sleeves.

Henry puts his drink down. 'I will come with you,' he says.

When he drops me off, he kisses me in front of the hairdresser. He tastes of Martini, but it's not sour or bitter like the one I drank at Glimmer. It's soft and hums across my tongue, warm and smooth. Maybe I've finally acquired a taste for gin.

'See you later.' Henry grins and walks away.

'Oh my God,' the hairdresser squeaks. 'He is *hot*!'

I smile and tuck my hair behind my ear. She ushers me over to a leather seat and drapes a cream gown over me. With Henry's kiss goodbye and my clothes covered, I relax and smile at my hairdresser.

'So, what are we doing today?' she asks, as though I see her every week.

'I was thinking about going red. Not bright red—'

'Copper,' she says, nodding as she runs her fingers through the lengths of my hair like she owns them. 'That will look great with your complexion. I'll go get your colour mixed.' She squeezes my shoulders before she walks away, and I relax. There are other girls getting their hair done for big nights out round London. Hairdryers buzz next to me and the sweet smell of hot styling products fills the air. There's a CCTV camera in the corner and I wonder if Henry's watching.

I grin at it and stick my tongue out. Of course he's watching.

After lightening my hair, the hairdresser leaves the cold red dye sinking into my scalp and my attention turns to the TV. A girl with dark hair is speaking with a reporter. I recognize her pointy chin and full lips. It's Emma. She's wearing a T-shirt, the scars along her right arm revealed by the short sleeve. Her mum pushes at her side, edging herself into the shot whilst flipping her hair over her shoulder. My stomach lurches at why Emma's being interviewed at all. It must be about me. I squint to read the subtitles on the bottom of the screen.

'This must be a very hard time for you both,' the reporter says. 'We understand from Scotland Yard that Mr Parry has been apprehended in the Cayman Islands.

Do you have any thoughts on the situation, Miss Parry?'

Emma nods. 'I'm just grateful he's not spent all the money and that people can get their pensions back.'

'Absolutely. I think they are just as grateful to have it returned,' the correspondent agrees. 'If you could say anything to your father, what would it be?'

Emma looks dead at the camera. 'Dad, if you're watching – I hope you rot in jail for what you've done.'

Mrs Parry shrieks a laugh. 'Careful, darling, we're on television. Goodness, where do children get these ideas from?'

'I'm not a child, Mum. I'm eighteen.'

The correspondent coughs and pulls the microphone away. 'Incidentally, Miss Parry, we understand you attend Grenville Academy. A girl from your year group – Lydia Phelps – is known to be missing from Grenville Psychiatric Unit. Did you know Lydia or care to comment?'

Emma is silent for a moment as she shifts in her seat. 'No. No comment. I didn't know Lydia very well.'

Mrs Parry frowns. 'But you—'

'I said we weren't friends,' Emma interrupts. 'I have no comment.'

The correspondent thanks Emma and her mother, ending the interview at the same time the hairdresser takes me to the sink to wash off my dye. As she massages my scalp, I think about how Emma hadn't commented on me despite having plenty to say. We treated each other badly but it feels like we might have reached an understanding.

EIGHTEEN

On my way back up to the room, I realize Henry's not given me a key card. I stand outside the door, but it clicks open without my knocking. Henry is sitting on the sofa when I walk in, his eyes distant as he hacks his way into something I can't see. He gets up and makes a big deal out of my hair. We look at it in the mirror together: it's sleek and shiny like a brand-new penny. He runs his hands through it and tells me how much he loves it.

I smile at him. 'Did you see the news?'

'Which channel?'

'One, I think. The interview with Emma?'

'Yes. Her father was caught and detained in the Cayman Islands.' Henry grins against my temple. 'I wonder who told her where to find him.'

I smile and relay the phone call I had with Emma when I was in Grenville Psych. Henry nods and then says, 'By the way, there is a surprise in the bedroom.'

I raise an eyebrow.

'The ASOS delivery has come.'

He laughs when I squeal and run into the bedroom, ready to throw anything on and bin my Grenville Psych outfit for good.

The bed is covered in black and white packages. Two new suitcases stand by the side.

'Henry, you've bought half the website!'

'I wanted you to be able to choose your own outfits,' he says with a quiet smile.

My heart twists at how he listened to me earlier. This is part of his apology for telling me what to wear before, and I'm seized by the idea of calling Dr Madison to tell her she was wrong.

'Thank you.'

'You are welcome.'

I turn to the bed and rip the packages open, tear off the plastic from each piece of clothing and hold it up against me. Henry's thought of everything, not just everyday clothes. There's pyjamas, underwear, shoes and matching bags. There's also a load of make-up I'm sure Henry will be better at using than me. We both turn away as I wrench my clothes off and throw them to the side. I slip into a pair of checked flannel pyjama shorts and an off-the-shoulder grey jumper. My fingers stroke the fabric, loving the soft feel of something new. I revel in the sensation of being cosy again after being cold and alone for so long.

I turn back and Henry's put on a dark-blue button-down shirt and some grey trousers. The fit accentuates his broad shoulders and I can see the bumps of his collar-bones peeking out of the unbuttoned neck. He's styled his hair differently while I was at the salon. There's more gel in it, a severe side parting I want to tangle my fingers in and muss. I watch him while he's not looking and think how much he is Henry. I spent so long wondering what he might look like. Now he's here, in front of me, I couldn't picture him as anyone else. I realize that's what kept me hammering away at creating him: I saw the personality he could be. It was Henry who evolved himself into the man in front of me. For me.

He hands me my next surprise.

A passport.

I open it and my heart flutters. I'm twenty-one, and my picture has red hair. But it's my name that catches my eye. Hall, Lydia Jane.

I throw my arms around his neck. I can't hold in the sob that pushes its way up my throat. Henry picks me up and carries me to the bathroom. He sets me on the counter and strokes my hair as he cradles me.

'Why are you crying, Lyd?'

'When I was in Grenville Psych I never thought I'd see you or your chip again,' I say, my voice muffled against his chest. 'I thought I'd lost your program, that I'd have to recreate you, but I knew I'd never be able to. Now you're here, looking after me and promising me the future we dreamt of before everything went crazy.' I look up to meet his eyes. 'You're here.'

Henry pulls me back into himself. His warm arms encircle my frame, making me feel small and safe. 'I said I would never leave you,' he says, chest rumbling.

As my tears subside, Henry produces a black wire from his pocket. 'I also ordered this.'

I've seen a wire like this before, days ago that seem like years ago. I grimace when I look at it. I remember how badly things went when the last wire was involved, and I wonder what Henry has planned. He undoes his shirt cuff and unwraps the bandage on his forearm to reveal a jagged line where I'd made the cut to ram Henry's chip in. It's still healing but he reopens it, making a small nick with a razor blade. I push his arm away from me as blood wells there, taking a deep breath to control the lurch in my stomach. He turns away to slide the wire inside, and winces before holding the other end up.

'Please will you link with me?'

'Can you be in more than one body?'

'Yes.' He nods. 'I have updated my program. We can talk inside your head as we used to.'

I hesitate to give him my arm. It was quiet without Henry in my head, and I did miss him, but now that he has his own body it feels nice to talk to him how I would with anyone else. But Henry still has much to learn if he's ever going to be human. The best way to teach him is to link with him. I peel my sleeve back and offer him my arm. 'I've missed you in my head. It's quiet without you.'

He lifts my chin and plants a kiss on my lips. 'It is quiet without you too.'

I take a moment to steady myself before I let him cut the skin above my elbow, reopening the wound there with steady hands. When I was in Grenville Psych I had treasured the mark where we were once linked, used to run my fingers over it a thousand times a day to remind me of him. Now he's reopening it to rejoin us. He eases the wire into the incision, and I inhale as the tendrils feel their way through my veins. They travel up my arm, searching for the chip.

When they find it, I jolt. A shooting pain screams up my nerves and into the base of my skull. Then a wave of thoughts run through my brain that aren't mine. It's a buzz of feelings, scattered words and whole sentences all at once. It's Henry. The noise of his mind recedes as he erects his barriers as before, and I can concentrate once more.

Hi, he says in my head. The chip in my arm buzzes, making me smile. I've missed it. *So long as I am near you, I can talk with you and show you things on your contacts.*

'My contacts!'

Henry hands a new pair to me. When I rip the foil from each packet, I see bright-green irises printed on the silicone. I turn around to the mirror to put them in and blink a few times to adjust. Henry smiles behind me in the mirror. Red hair and green eyes.

'I look like I've fallen out of a comic book,' I say. 'All I'm missing are the freckles.'

Henry grins and projects freckles on to my contacts. I laugh as I see them appear on myself in the mirror.

You look gorgeous, he says, and the freckles disappear. He kisses the back of my head and rests his chin on top of it. My green eyes wash over him. His hair is deep-black and shiny, continued in thick eyebrows and along the strong arms that wrap around me. The dark shirt complements his tanned skin. His eyes lock with mine. Summer-sky blue.

'I am sorry about the blue eyes, Lyd.' His smile falters as he reads my mind.

'It's just a colour,' I say, shaking my head. 'Dr Madison, she actually helped me get over a few things.' I turn around to look at Henry properly. 'What's it like with, you know – *him* in your head?'

Henry shrugs. 'It is a bit like having a split personality, except his part will never have control of the body. He will go away eventually.' He chuckles to himself, eyes distant. 'Oh, he did not like hearing that.'

'Good. He tried to blackmail me and then locked me up in Grenville Psych while he tried to break into your chip.' I look him in the eyes as I talk, knowing Agent Hall can hear me and has no ability to react. 'He deserves all he gets.'

I think about when Henry would talk in my head over someone who was talking to me in person. I'd never mastered hearing two voices at once. 'Isn't it confusing having more than one voice talking to you?' I ask.

Henry's smile tugs to the left. 'I can process more than your brain can. Sorry, Lyd. It does not bother me.' He looks down at the wire between us. 'Ready to take this out?'

I nod and grit my teeth as Henry yanks the wire tendrils from the chip like he's ripping off a plaster. I wrap tissue around the cut that bleeds anew. Henry does the same to his forearm, releasing a loud breath through his teeth once the wire is out.

He looks down at me. *I am still here,* he says in my head.

I stand on my tiptoes to kiss him and then he leaves me so I can have a shower. I don't ask him to go, but he's used to not being with me in the bathroom.

I tie my new hair back and lather up the over-perfumed jasmine shower gel as much as it will go, smothering it over my body. I wash away my stay in Grenville Psych and the choices that landed me there, trying my best not to dwell on what happened to Pete. All I can do now is move forward. Help Henry be the best person he can be. I wonder if he knows how badly I want him.

The bathroom door opens and clicks shut.

'Henry?' I can't see through the steam.

Henry pulls the shower door open behind me. I turn to face him. He's trembling slightly, and he bites his lip. His blue eyes are heated, churning like a broiling ocean. They never leave my face.

He heard my thoughts, I realize. He came to me because he wants me too.

Lydia, he says in my head.

It's a question. A plea for my permission, and it makes me shiver. I respond by pulling him into the shower. His clothes are soaked in seconds, but neither of us care. He ducks his head and kisses me. It's the kind of kiss that lights up my spine and breaks my skin out in goose-bumps. The kind of kiss that cements into my memory and I know will stay with me till my dying day.

'Please,' I whisper.

Henry's lips move to the curve of my neck. He kisses the skin there and his arms wrap around me. I bring my hands to his chest, trace over his smooth hard collarbones and unshaven jawline. His scent comes to me in layers. Underneath the sandalwood there's something spicy and masculine. It's Henry all over. I kiss his neck, desperate to taste him and know all of his secrets like he knows mine.

As I unbutton his shirt and slip it from his shoulders, I can't help but stare at his chest and the muscles that ripple down to his belt. He steps out of his trousers and closes the shower door. His hands graze over my hips, move to my ribs. He backs me against the slick tiles and hoists me up with a growl. Intuition takes over and I close my legs around his waist.

When our bodies meet, I cry out and bury my face in his neck. Henry holds me until pain gives way to pleasure and our bodies are transformed under the streaming water.

Henry leans one arm against the tiles and the other holds me to him. My ear is pressed to his heart. Every beat of it makes me love him more, makes me realize what he's done for me.

'Thank you for rescuing me.'

'Thank you for bringing me to life,' he whispers.

I shake my head against his chest, listen to the thump of his heart. 'You brought me to life,' I say. 'I love you, Henry. Do you know that?'

Henry clutches me closer to him. I can feel him sweep through every corner of my mind as he holds me, strokes my spine while the steam curls around our bodies. My breaths are shallow as I wait for his reply. I'm half expecting him to give me an answer composed of ones and zeros or an explanation of the limitations to his code.

'I love you too, Lydia.'

Warmth coils into my chest at his words. No one's ever said them to me before and I'm surprised at how filling they feel, yet how hungry they make me for more.

With a handful of words, Henry has far outstripped the program I sat down to create three years ago. If Henry is capable of love it means he's reached a level of sentience I never anticipated. The idea he was ever comparable to something that can't feel is wrong, because he *can* feel. Does feel. He's become more than some people will ever be. But after everything I've dealt with at Grenville Psych, there's one question that burns the back of my throat.

'What about guilt? Do you ever feel guilty?'

'Guilt is something I am unfamiliar with,' he says, making my insides twist. 'But I do feel sorrow over your time at Grenville Psych. I look over your memories and I see how you struggled, doubted yourself. I do not like that you were left there all on your own without me.'

I nestle against his chest. He is capable of feeling, but if he feels guilty over trying to take Pete's body, he doesn't show it. But I know he loves me, and that's enough to work with.

'I need you to be a better person for me,' I say. 'Can you do that?'

'I will do anything for you, Lyd. You know that.'

I smile. 'I know.'

'Do you want to hack something?' he asks after a while.

'Always.'

We lie on the bed together, staring at the ceiling. I glance over at Henry. His eyes are glassy and his blue irises flicker as he pulls information to his contacts. He projects it on to mine as well. He's pulling up everything he can find about Agent Andrew Hall, but he stops short after a birth certificate.

I expected more. Dental records, medical history, bank accounts. Henry is a better hacker than just a birth certificate.

'There is nothing else,' Henry says in my head. 'This is all I can find.'

'That's impossible, there must be more.' I sit up, watching as Henry hacks and rehacks, looking, searching for anything he can find.

'He has no digital trail, Lyd. There is only a birth certificate.'

I look at the hand in mine and wonder who it truly belongs to. Agent Hall had come to school looking for whoever hacked into IBI. He had the power to lock me away in a psychiatric unit. Someone like that has to have more than a birth certificate to their name. The body lying next to me suddenly feels very faceless. Is Andrew Hall even his real name?

'It does not matter,' Henry tells me as he reads my thoughts. 'I can still take care of it.'

He draws up a death certificate by hacking a local GP surgery, copying the details down as they appear elsewhere, changing the name and transferring a doctor's digital signature to the new certificate. For the cause of death, Henry writes *myocardial infarction*. He sends it to be certified by a Registrar and tells me he's not expecting any further issues.

'We do not have to worry about him any more, Lyd,' Henry says, and closes the hack. He rolls over. His weight presses against me. He kisses my nose, my chin, my neck, making me laugh. We stay up all night talking. And not talking.

NINETEEN

The body next to me stirs, waking me. Henry rolls from the bed. I listen, half asleep as he punches a number into the phone on the bedside table and murmurs a few words my sleep-addled ears can't make out. He stands up and faces away.

'Henry?'

He turns around and I can see his eyes are wrong. They're the same crystal blue, but they're narrowed. Simmering. He leaps across the bed and he's on me in a second. His hands grab at my throat. I scream but it comes out garbled. His thumbs press against my windpipe, squashing it into submission.

'H–enry!'

'Not any more, Phelps,' he hisses.

My legs kick under the crushing weight. I try to bring my knees up to whack him in the back, but Agent Hall bears down, his eyes locked on mine as he tightens his grip around my throat.

'We talk to each other, me and your body-snatcher boyfriend,' he drawls. 'I tell him all the ways I could hurt you and he tells me he'll do worse to me if I ever try.' He laughs in my ear as he leans forward and presses harder on my neck. 'But he's not here, is he?'

I can't breathe. My head feels hot and there's a pressure building behind my eyes. I give up scratching at his hands and move to the delicate area between his straddling legs. I pinch the wrinkly skin there, yanking on it hard. Hall yelps, and his hands flinch away. I kick him off and he falls to the floor with a gasp.

Air screams back into my lungs. I heave it in and scramble over the bed, kicking off the sheets that tangle around my legs. I fall to the floor and crawl to the bathroom where I lock myself in. Agent Hall hammers against the door a second later, the movement jerking through me as I lean against the wood.

'Get out here, you bitch! I'm gonna kill you!'

'Henry!' I scream. 'Get a grip on him!'

I sit against the door, gulping air. I can't hear Henry in my head. My mind is as quiet as it was in Grenville Psych. Agent Hall continues to batter against the door, throwing his weight against it. Once. Twice. Three times. The lock shakes, threatens to burst.

There's an emergency cord next to the toilet. If I pull it, someone will call the phone on the wall and I can yell for help. I make my way to it on my hands and knees, blood pounding through my ears. As I'm about to reach for the cord, the thudding against the bathroom door stops.

Silence descends. Tension pools in my bladder.

'Lydia?'

My breath catches as a wave of thoughts and images wash through my mind.

Lyd, it is me, Henry says in my head.

It's over. I collapse on the floor. *Henry, what the hell was that?* I say in my head. I go to the door and unlock it. Henry stands before me with wide eyes.

I am so sorry, Lyd. He tries to draw me into himself, to wrap his arms around me, but I shake him off.

'What happened?'

He ignores my attempts at batting him away, and his hands come to my jaw to trace the tender skin of my neck. He frowns as he looks it over. 'I was updating my program. I thought if he was asleep he might not notice me gone.'

'Are you insane? That was a really bad idea!'

'I am sorry. You never used to notice when I updated while you were asleep. He is more resilient than I thought.'

'He could have killed me!' I finger my neck. It's sore to swallow and I don't need a mirror to tell me it's going to swell like a bloated grape. Henry tugs at his boxers and winces. It must still hurt where I'd grabbed Agent Hall in my attempt to get him off.

'I'm not sorry,' I say, letting out a short laugh.

'I suppose I deserve it.' Henry pulls me to him. His heartbeat is calm, solid. I close my eyes and listen to its rhythm. It's Henry's.

His hands grip my shoulders. *Something is wrong*, he says in my head.

'What?'

'Agent Hall. He called someone.' Henry frowns as he mines the information from Agent Hall's brain. 'He called SSP. We have to get out of here.'

There's a crash as the bedroom window shatters. A canister lands on the bed, and I yelp as a white cloud bursts into the room. Henry guides me into the living room. He kicks the bedroom door shut and I grab cushions from the sofa to block the bottom of the door, so the gas can't seep through.

'Tear gas,' Henry says. 'They crept up on me. They are running silent to avoid my detection.'

'Who is?'

SSP, Henry says in my head. His eyes flicker as he stares out the window. Skyscrapers glitter back at us. *They have come for us.*

'What are you doing?' I ask, seeing his irises flash as he watches something I can't see.

'Learning hand-to-hand combat,' he replies. 'The same way I learnt how to do your make-up.'

I swallow, wondering if it will really come down to fighting for our lives, then remember how Agent Hall locked me away in a psychiatric unit. SSP mean business. And if Henry can master my make-up in a blink then I'm sure he can learn to defend us just as skilfully.

'Don't kill anyone.'

'Lydia—'

'No. They're people, Henry. Don't forget what you promised me.'

He nods, and his eyes clear. 'No killing.'

Glass splinters over the carpet as two agents smash their way through the living-room window. I scream and shrink against the bedroom door. Henry is on them in a second, legs kicking and hands dealing punches. Their padded armour reminds me of an American SWAT team from a film, but it works against them, bulky and constraining. They try to grab Henry, but he ducks and twists out of their way in a feral dance. His arms deliver sharp jabs and thrusts, aiming for the unguarded patch at the base of their necks.

One of the agents goes down at a punch from Henry, and I shriek as another bursts through the front door. I crawl behind the bar and grab at the bottles of alcohol stashed there. There's one shaped like a skull and I fling it across the room. It smashes against the helmet of the intruder. He swears and stumbles towards me.

Henry continues his assault of punches and kicks; he's a blur of limbs, jumping over furniture or pushing it in the way of his attacker.

I follow his lead and continue to throw bottles at the man coming towards me. A bottle of gin smashes at his feet and the scent of juniper fills the air. He grins under his helmet and chases me around the far side of the bar. My heart pounds in my throat but my mouth is dry. I've just escaped Agent Hall's clutches and now I have to deal with another maniac. The SSP agent leaps over the bar and I back away.

There's a rush of pumping wind and the deafening thump of machinery from the window. I chance a look and see the dark shape of a helicopter slide between the buildings and line up with our balcony. Air thrusts into the room and whips my hair around my face. My attacker takes his chance and tackles me to the floor.

Henry! I scream in my head.

He doesn't look my way, but outmanoeuvres his opponent with a dive that sends him flying into the TV. The screen smashes on impact, and the agent lies unconscious on the floor. The helicopter whines as it sidles up next to the hotel. I can see two more men inside getting ready to jump on to the balcony.

The SSP agent is thrown off me and into the bar behind him. Henry picks me up from the floor and holds me close. As he blinks, the helicopter's blades falter. An alarm drones from the cockpit as it loses altitude and begins to fall to the ground. The men inside scramble to get to their seats as they slip down the length of the deck towards the cockpit.

I wonder if Henry will fly it into the pavement and send all the people on board down with it. I've told Henry twice not to take a life, I can't tell him again. He needs to decide for himself.

The helicopter hangs at the side of the hotel, hovering in limbo as Henry decides what to do with it. His fingers tighten around me. I cringe as I wait for the ear-splitting crunch of metal meeting pavement, but it never comes.

The thump of the blades increases as the helicopter rises beyond our building and flies away over the city.

'Where are you sending them?'

'As far away as their fuel will take them.'

The tight knot that had been gathering in my chest fades. Henry made the right choice. It's a better resolution than a pile of metal and dead bodies.

'Thank you.'

'I can see who you want me to be, Lydia. And I see who you do not want me to be.'

'What did SSP want?' I say.

'Me. And you to tell them how you built me. Agent Hall rang them and told them where we were. Slippery bastard.'

I've never heard Henry swear before.

'Sorry,' he says, reading my mind. 'He called SSP, attacked you and deliberately tried not to think about the phone call in order to keep us at the hotel long enough to get us captured.' Henry slams the heel of his palm against the bar. 'It will not happen again.'

Agent Hall's anonymity tugs at me. He called for backup and SSP responded with armed men and helicopters.

'What can we do?'

Henry sets his jaw. 'It is time to end SSP. I was going to wait until we were further away, but now will have to do. They will be lucky if they can even load a USB stick after I have finished with them.'

Before, I would have jumped at the chance to hack

into something owned by someone who was trying to hurt us. I'd have sat back and watched Henry rip into their digital life and let him delete, rewrite. Ruin. I reach to hold Henry's hand, smooth and warm. He's here now. All I wanted for so long was his presence and now that I have it, I don't care about anything else.

'Maybe we should just leave,' I say. 'You can stop SSP from following us.'

'It is better to deal with them now.'

'But we could run away,' I insist.

Henry's blue eyes focus on me in a way that makes me shiver. 'I am not your father,' he says. 'I will not run.'

The declaration makes me swallow. I'd asked him to be a better person, but I never thought about myself. He's right. If we run now, we're no better than Dad. He'd told me to work through my problems, but he never worked on his own. If we deal with SSP now, we won't ever have to worry about them again.

'All right. So long as you—'.

'I will not kill anyone, Lyd.'

My contacts flick into life as Henry projects the hack on to them so I can see what he's doing. He traces the number that was on the BBC News and it leads to a building in London. He's inside before I can take a breath, streams of code appearing over my left eye, cameras appearing on my right. We cycle through rooms filled with desks and computers, server towers, boxes of components and parts.

He's inside their servers now, tearing through the

firewall to get into the software and hardware at the same time. I watch on the camera in the server room as he blows fuses and overloads wires that link the office computers to their network.

The flood of code on my left contact stutters.

'Henry?'

'Something is wrong.' Henry frowns as the code stops, his hack coming to an end. In a blink, it restarts. But it's different. Moving too fast, uncontrolled. This isn't Henry. I catch snippets of words as the code whizzes past my eyes. It's a virus.

Henry's mouth opens, and his hands come to his head as he cries out. The chip in my arm jerks, sending a sharp pulse into my brain that makes me gasp. Henry's thoughts are crashing waves. I can read his mind the same way he reads mine for a split second. The virus was encoded just for him. SSP anticipated an attack. They'd gleaned enough information from his chip to devise a fail-safe if Henry ever proved uncontainable. Henry's hack had sought to overload SSP's servers, but in doing so he activated the virus and it fed back to him through his own port of entry.

Underneath it all I can hear a laugh. It's cold and wild. Agent Hall is waiting, lingering in the background until he can regain control.

'I will . . . shut down . . . my link to you,' Henry gasps out.

The information on my contacts is ripped away and my mind goes silent, as if someone has switched off a loud TV. I look at Henry. His teeth are gritted, forehead screwed up. His arm jerks and a hand locks around my bicep. His blue eyes meet mine.

'Run,' he hisses.

Ice-snakes through my veins. I back away as Henry sinks to the ground. He trembles and gasps. I'm a few strides away when I pause. It would have been easy for Henry to run but he'd wanted to stay and do the hard thing, face the threat.

In the back of my mind, I watch my dad get into his car and drive away. I'd held my hand out to him – begged him to come back to me with everything that made me his. This whole time I'd thought I was like Dad because we look the same, share a love for computers. But that doesn't make us the same.

I run to Henry and hold his face to mine. 'I'm not my dad either,' I say. 'I won't leave you the way he left me. We're a team. Fight it, Henry. You can handle it.'

His teeth grind together, and a sheen breaks out across his forehead.

'I have to relinquish control of Hall,' Henry gasps. 'Only way . . .' He pushes me away and I fall to the floor. 'Run!'

'No,' I say, fighting tears. 'I won't leave you. I lost you once, I won't lose you again.'

There's a loud beating in the distance. Without Henry to tell it where to go, the helicopter must have regained control and has returned.

'Henry!' I try to pull him to the door by his armpits but

he's too heavy. He thrashes, fighting to maintain control over Agent Hall, and he falls back down. His hands are pressed against his temples. The TV flickers and dies and the lights flash on and off.

My heart hammers as the door swings wide and even more agents than before pour in. One of them steps towards me, arms out as though to try to calm me down. I back away as he comes for me. A female agent murmurs into her phone and the thump of the helicopter becomes louder than ever. Henry cries out on the floor. Two SSP agents descend from wires and land on the balcony. They point their assault rifles at Henry.

We're surrounded.

Kneeling down, I kiss Henry on his cheek and inhale his warm scent. 'I won't leave you.' Hands encircle my arms and haul me away from him.

When I was arrested in Glimmer, I'd kicked and screamed and struggled the whole way to the police car. Now I'm calm as I'm escorted out of the hotel and strapped into the carriage of the helicopter. Henry is secured to the floor. Wherever SSP are taking us, we're being taken together and that's good enough for me. Henry writhes in his restraints, fighting a war on two fronts – defeating the virus and holding on to Agent Hall.

There's an agent on either side of me, and another with red hair sits opposite. He hands me some ear defenders which blanket out most of the noise of the chopping blades. My stomach rolls as we start to ascend and the buildings shrink beneath us.

The red-headed agent looks down at Henry writhing from side to side, grin wide and pointy. 'Looks like your boy here's struggling with something.'

'What did you do to him?'

'You'll have to wait till we get to HQ to find out.'

I lean down to hold Henry's hand. His fingers are clammy against mine, his grip too tight. I'm not sure if it's Henry trying to hold on, or Agent Hall trying to crunch my bones.

I ignore the pain and look out over the concrete capillaries of London. We look to be descending towards a blocky, unadorned grey building I recognize from Henry's earlier hack. I never noticed before but, in person, it has zero architectural charm, not even windows. It's a solid concrete block. Even Grenville Psych had windows, despite having bars over them. This is nothing like that.

'Come on, Henry,' I say in my head. 'I need you.'

TWENTY

enry is separated from me when we enter the building. I don't know where he is taken and none of the agents respond to me when I ask. I'm led by the elbow through several white corridors and pushed through a door into a pale room with stale air and no windows. A man with a receding hairline and grey eyes sits at a table. The red-headed agent plonks me in the seat opposite him and leaves.

'Hello, Miss Phelps. I'm Agent Dixon,' the man says.

'What do you want?'

'It's very good to finally meet you in person,' he says, as if I have greeted him warmly. 'Agent Hall had you on his radar for some time. He promised me you were one of the best programmers he'd ever come across. We see now that his observations were correct.'

'I have nothing good to say about Agent Hall in return,' I snap. 'Tell me what you want.'

'Very well,' Agent Dixon says with a nod. 'I need your

help. Our fate as a species will be determined by our ability to harness the potential of Artificial Intelligence and SSP needs to be at the forefront of this movement. Do you have any idea what it is you've created? Your AI is akin to that rare book produced when one million monkeys hammer away at one million typewriters for one million years.'

'His name is Henry. And he's a person, not a thing.'

'Henry is dangerous,' Agent Dixon retorts. 'I am sure you're aware of how he is capable of doing anything he wants?'

I shift in my seat. I haven't forgotten how Henry could have killed a handful of people by now if I hadn't put a stop to it. Without guilt, he's comparable to a psychopath. 'He won't hurt anyone. He promised me.'

'Yes . . .' Agent Dixon's eyes rake over me. 'He seems particularly invested in you. Why is that?'

'Why does anyone do anything? Henry can make choices like anyone else.'

'But he doesn't have the morals you and I have. He's not a complete person, is he?'

Henry has particular tastes – tastes I don't share. I don't like coffee or gin, but he does. He knows what he likes just as any other person does. Just because Henry hasn't fully learnt morals yet doesn't mean he's not capable of them.

I lean back in my chair. Whatever Dixon wants, it isn't a conversation. 'I don't think you brought me here to debate ethics surrounding AI,' I say.

'Quite right. To the point, then.' Agent Dixon pushes a pad of yellow paper and a pen towards me. 'You are the only person I know who can design what we want, and we're willing to do you a deal. We have infected Henry with a virus. It's the digital equivalent of dementia. Currently, it's ripping its way through his systems quicker than he can rewrite them, which is saying something.' He holds his hand up to silence my interruption. 'I'll give you the cure for the virus, but we want something in return. You have to work with us. Teach us to build another AI.'

I look at the notepad that can't be more than thirty sheets of paper and let out a laugh. My bedroom was covered in pages, diagrams, maps. Some of the algorithms continued on to the walls in Sharpie. The floor was a carpet of circuit boards and wires, chips and cards plugged together.

'I'll need a computer.'

Agent Dixon raises an eyebrow. He's not stupid enough to put me in front of a computer. 'I think not, Miss Phelps. You will have to make do.'

'I didn't sit down one day and write out his program. It took me three years,' I say. I want to say I had help – Dad encouraged me when I learnt to code, but it was only over my shoulder. Henry is more mine than he ever was Dad's.

Dixon pushes on, saying, 'Then may I suggest you hurry up?'

I swallow at the bluntness of it all. 'And if I refuse?'

Agent Dixon meets my eye. 'That would not be recommended. You have what I want and I have what you want. I'm not a monster, Miss Phelps, but I know what motivates you and I'm prepared to do what is necessary. Do you understand?'

He puts a laptop on the table and turns it my way. On screen, there's a doctor's office with floor-to-ceiling bookshelves and a forest-green carpet. Two people sit on a chesterfield.

'What's Henry like? Your boyfriend.' Dr Madison asks.

'He's protective,' I say after a minute, voice tinny through the laptop speakers.

'What does he do that's protective?'

'He stands up for me when no one else will. He's always there.'

Dixon closes the screen. 'It's clear to me that you are just as protective over him. After all, you were willing to go to a psychiatric unit to protect him. Yes?'

I glare at him. I'd thought it was Agent Hall who was watching me, but I realize now SSP's involvement went far deeper. Hall was a cog in a machine, and I kick myself for focusing on him. Henry saw the bigger picture. He'd tried to deal with it, and it all went wrong. The virus has brought him to his knees. Dixon knows how vulnerable he is at the moment.

I take a shaky breath. 'What kind of AI would I be programming?'

'We need a gatekeeper. Someone to watch for rogue viruses and programs designed to infiltrate our country. Your AI would help us track potential threats, help us block attacks from other countries and identify where they come from. Forget nuclear, Miss Phelps, forget chemical weaponry. It's cyberattacks we need to worry about now. AI wars are inevitable. We need to be prepared for them.'

'So you don't want another Henry?'

'Not exactly. We want something *like* Henry,' he says. 'Sentient enough to work intelligently but that can ultimately be controlled. Limited by Asimov's Three Laws of Robotics.'

I shake my head. 'Anything I build for you will eventually become self-aware and evolve like Henry did. They will choose whether to follow the rules or not. I can't force them to obey.'

Agent Dixon sits back as he considers this. 'Perhaps the issue of how we control it is a conversation for another time. We will settle for your teaching us how to build one.'

Everything in me screams about how little choice I have and how Henry is already ruined, possibly irreparably, because of this man. And here he is lecturing me about how dangerous Henry is when it's *him* who is holding Henry's cure to ransom.

'I'll leave you to consider my offer, and it might be best if you had something to show me when I return.' Dixon gets up to leave.

'You can't leave me in this cell!' I say, turning to him. 'You're not the bloody government, I . . .' I pause as Agent Dixon throws me a patronizing smile. Everything clicks into place: why Agent Hall had corrected our IT teacher and said he was 'Mr Hall' to try and be less official, but he didn't even blink when I'd called him Agent Hall. He had the power to lock me in a psychiatric unit when I didn't do what he wanted. Why he had no records bar a birth certificate – an anomaly in a world where everyone has a digital footprint.

He wasn't just an agent working for a cybercrime company. He was a *government* agent. Henry must have known. He could read Hall's mind the way he can read mine, so he would have known exactly who Hall was, but he never told me. He tried to handle the problem on his own and it all went wrong.

'You *are* part of the government, aren't you?' I ask.

'We are one of their unofficial branches, yes,' Dixon says.

'You don't . . .' I trail off, thinking about how the media had hounded us. Armed guards and helicopters had come after us, tracking us as deftly as the military.

'Look after banks?' he finishes for me. 'Not so much as we monitor them for people like you who want to establish their reputation as a hacker. We are interested in those skill sets. The government is very keen to develop defences against the next generation of computers, but you did more than we could ever have hoped for by building Henry. My superiors are extremely interested in his design. Think about my offer, Miss Phelps. Henry's future is in your hands. I'll come back in an hour. If I like what I see, we'll talk about getting you a team to commence work.'

Dixon presses the yellow pad into my hands before leaving the room.

The anger I'd lidded since my escape from Grenville Psych boils over. I pick up the chair, ready to smash it against the table or throw it at the wall. My muscles scream to unleash the anger coursing through them. Instead, I put the chair down and sink to the ground, limbs trembling.

TWENTY-ONE

Agent Dixon's offer loops through my mind. I could try to design another AI in return for the cure, but that would mean another AI could become sentient under my guidance. And how long would it take? Henry took me three years, and I had help from Dad to begin with. There's no way Henry can wait that long for the cure.

If I coded something new, what would the result be, anyway? Henry doesn't hurt anyone because I've asked him not to, but whatever I create next may not be so willing to follow my instruction. It probably comes down to luck. I'm *lucky* that Henry turned out to be so wonderful. He's more than capable of tearing digital holes in the world, but he chooses not to because he's loyal to me. A rogue AI could quickly assert itself at the top of the food chain.

I hug the writing pad to my chest. Henry is the only one who's ever stood by me, ever promised me they'd never leave and kept that promise. He's the closest thing I have to family.

I can't see another way out.

I scribble down a few programs that I can remember, but it all feels useless without a computer. Most of the codes I worked on for months and I can't recall every piece of them. Single subroutines took days, weeks to perfect. Each part of Henry's personality was balanced in a spiderweb of programs. When he became sentient enough, he rewrote many of them. Dixon doesn't understand I only got Henry so far. Henry himself did most of the heavy lifting.

Lydia, Henry says in my head. His voice is like a whisper in the corner of my mind. I've never heard it this faint before.

'Henry? How – are you okay? Where are you?'

Close by, I think. I heard you yelling.

He doesn't say anything for a moment. I sit rigidly, willing my heartbeat to quieten as I wait for him to speak again.

I have found a way to slow the virus down but I cannot control Hall at the same time. It is just a matter of time . . .

Henry's voice is so quiet it could be my own thoughts playing tricks on me.

'I'm working on getting the cure from Dixon, Henry. I'm trying, I'm writing a new AI, but it might be a while. Do you think you can hold on?'

I hold my breath in the silence that follows. My eyes dart round the room as I search my mind for any hint of his voice.

I want to let the virus take me, he says.

'What do you mean?'

I am killing Agent Hall, Lyd. The longer I hold on the more damage I cause his body. His organs are failing because I cannot keep them running. I released control of him, and he attempted to remove my chip from his arm. It would be better to let the virus take me.

I stand up with a frown. 'But what does that mean for you?'

The virus is working its way into my centre. I will not be able to hold it off for much longer.

I shake my head as I realize what he's saying. 'So . . . you'll die?'

His voice is an echo that sweeps through my core and stirs every part of my soul. *Yes.*

'You can't! I won't let you,' I say, and swallow. 'You said you'd never leave me. I love you.'

But could you love a murderer? Could you look the other way while I manipulate this body for my own end? I am preventing him from being conscious. Is that not the same as killing him?

'It's only Agent Hall,' I say, sniffing as I think about how he imprisoned me and tried to kill me. He'd probably try again if given the chance. 'He's not worth saving.'

Life is life, Lyd. There is not one rule for Agent Hall and one rule for everyone else.

Tears slide down my face at the rightness of his argument. His overpowering of Agent Hall is no different to how he wanted to kill those agents back at the hotel. Henry was a personality before he had a body, fundamentally shaping his understanding of human life. Personality *is* life to Henry. Now he sees overtaking Hall's body as the same as killing him. I'd never thought of it that way before. We used him to our own end. What we did with his body at the hotel . . . no wonder he tried to kill me.

'This is different,' I tell him.

A chuckle pulses through my mind, and I suddenly hate how quickly Henry learns, how logical he is. He finally understands the right to live and it's not fair.

'You're all I have in the world, Henry. Please.'

I could take him, Lyd. But I do not want to. I feel . . . guilty that I did not do things properly before. It is the right thing to let the virus take me. It is what I deserve.

Everything blurs as my tears fall fast and steady. He's learnt to feel guilt and compassion. His respect for life makes him as human as me. He's become the man I wanted him to be and it's too late.

I did it for you, he whispers, reading my mind. *It has all been for you.* His invisible lips find mine for the lightest whisper of a kiss.

I press my fingers to my lips, to trace over his touch.

Dr Madison suggested Henry was a distraction for what was going on around me. Part of that is true, but I realize now it's more. I created Henry because I'd wanted someone to love and have love me back. Someone who'd never leave me the way so many people have. I may not have coded any of this into his program, but Henry picked up on it anyway.

He was the one to leap to my defence when he saw me being bullied. He was the one who fought at my side when I wanted revenge. He wanted to progress to a physical presence because that was what I needed: someone to hold me. Love me. As soon as he'd linked with me, he could see into the recesses of my mind and understood things before I consciously knew them. He knew I wanted a home and I wanted to be safe and protected, surrounded by people who wanted me.

The whole time I was in Grenville Psych I'd worried about Henry's morality and what he was capable of doing because he didn't show remorse. But Henry was never evil or malicious. All his actions were dictated by his desire to see me happy. I craved the home I'd lost, and Henry wanted to give it back to me.

Now, he sees I want him to be someone who values life, and that's what he's striving for. Even if it means leaving me. Even if it means falling on his own sword.

'Wait, Henry, this isn't what I want . . .'

He doesn't reply. Silence hums around me as I go to the door and scream as loud as I can, 'Let me out!'

No one comes.

I pound the door, try the handle over and over and over but it won't budge.

I claw at the hinges, at the bottom and the top of the door, where a box with a blinking red light—

There. I'm going to find Henry if it kills me. If Agent Hall is all that's left behind, he might literally try, but I don't care – can't care. Henry is all I have, and I won't let him go without trying. I won't leave him the way I have been left.

I drag the chair over to the door and stand on it to pull the cover off the access-control box. For a while, I let these things rule my life. Not today. I pull out reams of wires and yank them as hard as I can. There's a popping noise and the light fades to black. I push on the door, testing it, and nearly fall into the corridor beyond.

There are several doors near mine. Henry said he was nearby. I slink into the corridor and look through the window of each door – nothing but rooms filled with people. Agent Dixon almost spits his coffee out when he sees me. I run to the next door, but Dixon follows me out, flanked by other agents.

'Where is he?' I demand as they try to grab me. 'He's threatening to let the virus take him. If I lose Henry, I will never EVER give you what you want. Take me to him now or I'll take all my coding knowledge to my grave.'

Dixon's grey eyes blink at me behind his glasses. 'All right.' He nods to one of his agents. 'Let her see him.'

The agent goes to a door I hadn't yet checked and unlocks it with his pass. I barge past him, into a room similar to mine. The door clamps shut behind me, but I don't care about being locked in. Henry's on the far side, lying on the floor with his head turned to the wall.

I pull him towards me and shake him by the shoulder. 'Henry, it's me. Don't leave me. You have to stay, we promised we'd never leave each other. Please. I love you.'

Henry's eyes snap open and focus on me.

I palm away my tears as he sits upright.

'Henry?'

His summer-blue eyes narrow. 'Not any more, Phelps.'

I yelp as Agent Hall's hands come around my neck for the second time in as many days. Tendons ripple in his forearms from the force. I choke as he squashes me into the floor.

People shout in the background, but I don't hear them, don't register the clank of the door coming unlocked or the people rushing in to pry Hall away. He shakes them off, determined. He's really going to kill me. He hates me that much for what we did to him. I can see it in his eyes, the way they're tightened into slits and are focused on me and only me.

For the briefest of moments, they soften.

I love you, Lydia, Henry whispers in my head, *and I am sorry.*

Agent Hall's hands freeze around my neck. He falters and it's his turn to choke. One hand goes to his chest, to his heart. The agents surround him and wrestle him away. I scoot back, unsure what's going on. Hall cries out and I can see from his eyes something's not right. They're the same eyes Dad had before we crashed, filled with the knowledge that whatever is happening can't be controlled. He gasps, and his breathing turns shallow. His legs buckle.

The other agents swap a look. 'Medic!' one of them yells, and runs to the door. 'We need a medic!'

It's too late. Agent Hall is prone on the floor, chest unmoving.

'Henry?' I crawl over to him. His summer-sky blue eyes are glassy and unfocused. I slap his cheeks, but he doesn't move. I don't understand. He was just here. The virus had imprisoned him, but he was still alive. What did Henry do to Agent Hall?

Dixon grabs me as a medic rushes in and kneels at my side.

'Help him! You have to help him!' I scream at her.

She puts two fingers to Agent Hall's neck and shakes her head at Dixon. 'There's no pulse. Starting CPR. Get me a defibrillator,' she snaps at one of the agents and starts doing chest compressions. 'Sir? Sir, can you hear me?' She speaks loudly, clearly, but I almost don't hear her because my heart is hammering so loud the noise drowns everything else out.

An agent darts out of the room and reappears with a bright yellow box. The medic snatches it from his hands and starts to attach the defibrillator. My breath is tight in my lungs.

Agent Dixon pulls me away. I hadn't realized I'd crawled back to Henry's side. I watch, limbs locked tighter than a bank vault, as the medic follows the instructions the defibrillator issues out in a horribly calm and emotionless manner.

I twist my fingers. I pick at my nails. Henry has to survive. He just has to.

After a moment, the medic rocks back on her heels. She looks at Dixon with a grave expression. 'Defib can't help. He's ... gone.'

A scream rips from my throat and I struggle out of Dixon's arms. I push the medic away. She was no help at all. Henry's name is a wail on my lips. He doesn't respond, doesn't move. Doesn't even blink.

I sink to the floor next to Henry, crying out his name. I bury my face in his still-warm neck and inhale the spicy scent I knew would be there. Maybe if I smell it long enough, inhale it into my core and hold it there for ever, it won't ever leave me.

Someone approaches my side and reaches out to close Henry's eyes. I knock their hand away. 'Don't touch him!'

'Lydia . . .' Dixon kneels next to me. 'He's gone. They're both gone.'

I gasp at the reality of it all. 'This is all your fault!' I cry, and jab him on the arm. 'This is *all* your fault! You held his cure to ransom. You gave him no choice!' I slap at his chest, pound my fists against him until his arms wrap around me to force me to be still.

'I know he was all you had,' Dixon whispers. 'I know, I know.'

I hate how well he understands what Henry meant to me. He watched all my sessions with Dr Madison. He knew I had no one else. Henry was everything to me.

And it's his virus that killed him.

TWENTY-TWO

'It was a heart attack,' Dixon explains a day later. 'There was nothing anyone could have done.'

His gaze doesn't meet mine, and his unspoken accusation weights the air between us. Nineteen-year-olds don't just have heart attacks. Henry stopped Agent Hall's heart to save my life.

'Right,' I say weakly.

Dixon plays with his watch for a moment. 'This is why Henry was dangerous, Lydia. Do you see now? He was more machine than he was a person, no matter how complex his program was.'

Part of me wants to laugh, the other part wants to slap Dixon for being so callous. Henry was going to sacrifice his life to save Agent Hall. A machine would never do that because it would never understand why it should, it would only look out for itself. What's more, no matter how much he didn't want to kill Hall, he did it anyway because he loved me more. He made a choice. Henry's final act proves he was human.

Dixon doesn't seem to realize the only reason Henry had to act at all was because he was infected by the virus. He could have transferred back to me and we'd have left Hall alone. If Henry hadn't been infected, we'd have been in another country by now.

Tears slip from my eyes. It's not just the virus that destroyed Henry. I infected him on a much deeper level. He was striving to please me, to be everything I wanted him to be. The more human he became, the more I held him to a higher standard, and he tried so hard to live up to it that he chose to die.

Dixon pushes an anti-static bag across the table. 'We retrieved this for you,' he says. 'I thought you would want to have it.'

I take the chip and hold it to my heart. This chip used to send a thrill through me at the thought of how much power it held. What it contained. In the end, Henry was far more vulnerable than I ever could have realized. He should have used his last ounce of strength to keep the virus at bay but he used it to save my life instead.

'I guess it's useless to you now,' I say. 'The virus destroyed him so there's nothing left to pick apart.'

Dixon tries to smile but it's weak and off-centre. He knows I'm right. 'I'm very sorry, Phelps. I've arranged for a car to take you back to Grenville Psychiatric Unit.'

I watch as he leaves. Back to Grenville. A numb realization sinks in that I have nowhere else to go and this time, Henry won't be coming for me.

I fold the chip into my palm and bring it to my lips. Henry was the best person I ever knew, and probably always will be. That body belonged to him. Those summer-sky blue eyes capable of piercing through all the darkest corners of my heart were his and only his. His name, borrowed for a time, was his.

Hen-ry.

Hen-ry.

Hen-*ry*.

ONE MONTH LATER

I dream of both Henrys almost every night. One, I spin round and round my garden. The other, I run into a white room and see him lying against the far wall. No matter how fast I run, I can never get to him. The room elongates and he is forever out of my reach.

Dr Madison thinks this is positive. It's acceptance, she says. I nod along when she repeats her belief that Henry was controlling and ultimately no good for me. Her new theory is that I made something seemingly invincible to replace something so fragile and these dreams are my subconscious acceptance that they are both gone. I disagree. Both Henrys were vulnerable, just in different ways. They were very different people, in the end.

Mum leans over the table and pushes a photograph my way. My brother beams up at me as a snake coils around his shoulders, a zoo-related treat for his ninth birthday. I remember the day well, but I haven't seen the picture for years.

'I thought you could keep it,' she says. 'Put it in your room.'

'Thanks,' I say, and take it from her. She brings me something every week, and I know how hard it is for her to part with each item. Anything that Henry once touched she hoards in her room like she's some kind of dragon. I know this is more than just a picture to her.

'How's Pete?' I ask her every time I see her.

Mum's eyes flick away from me. 'I saw him in town the other day. He was on crutches. His mother shooed me away as soon as she saw me.'

Both guilt and relief wash over me. 'I'm sorry,' I say.

Mum's lip quivers. 'It's me who's sorry, Lydia. I'm sorry I let things get so bad.' She takes a breath to collect herself. 'I thought you'd become unhinged, talking to your brother like he was still here. Dr Madison told me what you did, what you built.' Her faded sky-blue eyes focus on me and only me for the briefest of moments. 'I knew you were clever but I had no idea you were *that* clever. You are so much like your father.'

'I'm nothing like him,' I say. The words come out harsher than intended but Mum only nods.

'I understand,' she says.

The buzzer goes, signalling the end of visiting hours, and I stand up as orderlies come in to take us all back to the ward. Mum gives me a hug. She gives me one every time we see each other. At first they were awkward, but they've become more natural now.

'See you next week,' she says.

'Eat something other than pizza,' I tell her. She smiles and waves me off.

I'm escorted back with the other girls, but as they're led through to the ward, Simon pulls me to one side. 'You have another visitor,' he says, and takes me to a smaller room, the one where Agent Hall once visited me.

When I'd last been here, streaks of blood – his and mine – had been smeared across almost every surface. Now it's clean, and Agent Dixon smiles from the other side of the table.

'Hello, Phelps,' he says.

Simon shuts the door behind me but departs with a look that tells me if I try anything, I'm in for it.

'What do you want?' I blurt.

'Sit down, please.' He indicates to the chair opposite his, still smiling as if he has invited me for tea and biscuits.

'How are you?' he asks as I sit down.

'Good,' I say, and find I'm only half lying.

'Excellent, excellent. I must confess to being here in a professional capacity and I don't have much time. Please forgive me, but I wondered if you would help me with something.'

I fold my arms as he brings out a laptop. I wonder if he's going to show me another snippet of myself talking to Dr Madison in one of our sessions, but when he swivels it my way, I'm faced with a block of code.

'What's this?'

'We've been having some trouble with this and I

wondered if you could make the program work for me. Please.' He pushes the laptop so it's right in front of me. My fingers come to the keyboard before I've told them to – as if they reflexively know where they belong.

The code is mine. Henry's. I recognize it straight away as I scroll through it. It's an expanded version of the small program I jotted down over a month ago when I was in SSP's headquarters. But it's wrong. They've done things to it, twisted it until it's almost useless.

'You know what's wrong with it, don't you?' Agent Dixon says. His grey eyes see far too much and not enough at the same time. He's not noticed the coding error near the beginning, or the one that's close to the end that means it'll crash whatever he uploads it to.

'Can you fix it?'

I nod and correct the code for him. It only takes five minutes. He blinks when I push the laptop back to him.

'You needed to move that last bit around,' I tell him. 'Otherwise it would've crashed.'

Dixon thumbs his bottom lip. 'We'd been struggling with that for a couple of days. It's set our project deadline back.'

'What are you building, Agent Dixon?' I ask, though I can guess. Why else would he be using my program?

'Top secret, I'm afraid. But, if you're interested, we could enrol you in SSP?'

'And become an agent, like you?' I ask.

'We need you, Phelps. You're the best programmer I've ever come across.'

'Does that mean I'll get a computer?'

Dixon smiles, and I smile back. I knew he would come here. It was only a matter of time.

'You can have five,' he says.

SIX MONTHS LATER

'Sally was asking after you.' Agent James Fielding runs a hand through his afro hair as he approaches me. 'What're you working on?'

He leans against the dividers separating our desks. I alt and tab my way to a different screen as he looks at it.

'Just updating an algorithm for SAL.'

'Sally was asking after you this morning,' he says again. 'She always does.'

'Its name isn't Sally,' I warn him. 'And watch your pronouns.'

He shrugs. 'Sentient Artificial Lifeform isn't very personal though, is it? Anyway, she's like a kid. Kids need names.' His gaze slips to his desk and I know he's staring at a picture of the sister he never talks about. He doesn't need to. I've been around that kind of thing long enough to know death when I see it.

'Don't call it Sally. Don't humanize it, James.'

His dark eyebrows rise. 'Is that the mistake you made,

Lyd?' My fingers stroke my keyboard as I ignore him. I wonder about seizing it and wrapping it around his forehead. 'I didn't mean— It's just everyone knows . . .'

I take a breath and smile instead. 'Do me a favour and give SAL its data chip today?' I ask. Anything to get rid of him so I can carry on with what I was doing.

'Sure. Unlike you, I don't need an excuse to see Sally.' He grins at me, so I know he's only teasing.

'SAL,' I correct.

He ignores me and wanders away. I flick back to my original screen. The office is otherwise empty, and I take advantage of it.

Code through the problem, Lydia. Not around it.

No matter how many times I told Dr Madison, she never understood how different Henry and my brother were. What's more, she never understood how fundamentally different their deaths were. People can't be revived, but AIs can. It's just a case of unravelling it all. All I needed was access to a computer and a server powerful enough to support a complex program. SSP provided both. All that needed tweaking was the sentinel software loaded on to my PC to log every keystroke I made. Now it only records one in ten keystrokes and is randomized to something else. The best they get from my PC is a pile of gibberish, but Agent Dixon can't argue that I'm not working. SAL reached sentience two months ago.

The only sound in the office is the click of my fingers over my keyboard.

I'm so close. So gut-wrenchingly close it makes me need to pee. A few more lines of code and I've finally finished unpicking the virus.

I press enter and hold my breath as a blinking white cursor blossoms on to the screen.

I gaze at the webcam built into the monitor. 'Henry?'

A word appears one letter at a time on my screen, as if invisible fingers are using my keyboard. *Lyd?*

The chip in my arm buzzes.

//End

ACKNOWLEDGEMENTS

Thank you:

To Joanna Moult for being the first person who said yes to me when fifty others said no, and for all your advice and guidance that followed afterwards.

To Kesia, Esther, Barry, Rachel L, Rachel H, Elinor, Sarah, Jazz, Laura and everyone at Chicken House for being the exact right place for Lydia and Henry, and for giving me such a wonderful home. To Sam Palazzi and all of Scholastic US for giving me a second. I'm endlessly grateful.

To Oli, who took me to writing lessons and listened to my stories. Who taught me to chase my dreams, cheered me on and poured me wine – both to celebrate and to commiserate – I love you.

To my parents: Dad, who bought me all the books I ever asked for, queued with me at midnight on *Harry Potter* release days, and generally filled my head with stories. And Mum, for being a tireless cheerleader, prayer warrior and a constant believer that this would happen for me.

To my #TeamSkylark buddies for being my community to fall back on. Guy Lucas, for being the best person to go drunk-book-buying with, Emily Lowrey for being the best camera-wielding author I know, and to Aislinn O'Loughlin for your endless enthusiasm, and for always talking to me like Henry and Lydia were real people. Also: GOATS. There, I got it in!

To StudioHelen and the Scholastic art department for bringing Henry and Lydia to two gorgeous covers I still can't believe are just for me. Thank you.

To God, whose timing will always be better than mine and whose promises continue to be yes and amen. Thank you, thank you, thank you.

To you, lovely reader. The publishing industry starts and ends with you, and I can't thank you enough for picking up my book.

THE LOOP by BEN OLIVER

Luka Kane will die in the Loop, a prison controlled by artificial intelligence. Delays to his execution are granted if he submits to medical experiments, but escape is made impossible by the detonator sewn into his heart.

On Luka's sixteenth birthday, the monotony of life in the Loop alters: the government-issued rain stops falling and rumours of outside unrest start to spread.

This might be his one chance to escape – and to stop the deletion of humankind . . .

A terrifying and sinister look into the future that will leave your jaw on the floor.
KASS MORGAN, AUTHOR OF *THE 100*

Paperback, ISBN 978-1-912626-55-7, £7.99 • ebook, ISBN 978-1-912626-61-8, £7.99

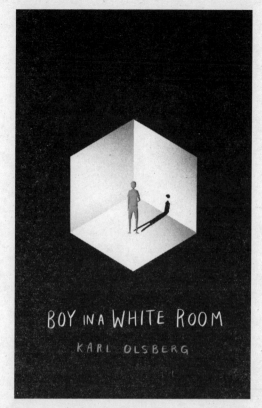

BOY IN A WHITE ROOM by KARL OLSBERG

A fifteen-year-old boy wakes to find himself locked in a white cube-shaped room. No windows, no doors, total silence.

He has no memories, no clue how he got there – and no idea who he is.

As the boy uncovers snippets of his story – an attempted abduction, a critical injury, a murder – it becomes clearer. But when some of the pieces don't fit, how can he tell what's real and what's not? Who can he trust? And who is he really . . . ?

Paperback, ISBN 978-1-912626-22-9, £7.99 • ebook, ISBN 978-1-913322-46-5, £7.99

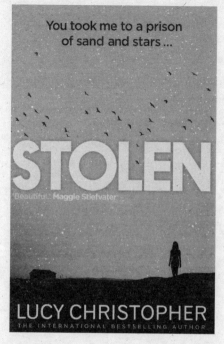

STOLEN by LUCY CHRISTOPHER

It happened like this.

I was stolen from an airport.

Taken from everything I knew, everything I was used to. Taken to sand and heat, dirt and danger. And he expected me to love him. This is my story.

A letter from nowhere.

A vivid new voice for teens.
MELVIN BURGESS

Tautly written and hard to put down.
INDEPENDENT ON SUNDAY

Paperback, ISBN 978-1-908435-75-0, £7.99 • ebook, ISBN 978-1-908435-18-7, £7.99

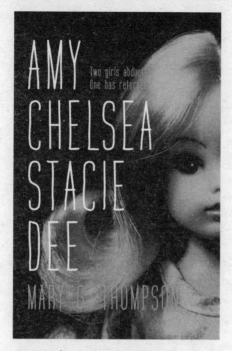

AMY CHELSEA STACIE DEE by
MARY G. THOMPSON

A stranger took Amy and Dee as children and gave them new names. Now at sixteen and called Chelsea, Amy has returned. Dressed in purple and clutching a plastic doll, she refuses to answer questions but locked inside her is the truth. How did she survive? Why did she escape? And what happened to Dee?

Constantly kept me guessing. One of the best YA books I've ever read — I regularly force it into people's hands.
C.J. SKUSE

Paperback, ISBN 978-1-910655-81-8, £7.99 • ebook, ISBN 978-1-911077-31-2, £7.99